LINE OF DUTY

FOG LAKE SUSPENSE, BOOK 4

CHRISTY BARRITT

COMPLETE BOOK LIST

Squeaky Clean Mysteries:

#13 Cold Case: Clean Getaway

#14 Cold Case: Clean Sweep

#15 Cold Case: Clean Break

#16 Cleans to an End (coming soon)

While You Were Sweeping, A Riley Thomas Spinoff

The Sierra Files:

#1 Pounced

#2 Hunted

#3 Pranced

#4 Rattled

The Gabby St. Claire Diaries (a Tween Mystery series):

The Curtain Call Caper

The Disappearing Dog Dilemma

The Bungled Bike Burglaries

The Worst Detective Ever

#1 Ready to Fumble

#2 Reign of Error

#3 Safety in Blunders

#4 Join the Flub

#5 Blooper Freak

#6 Flaw Abiding Citizen

#7 Gaffe Out Loud

#8 Joke and Dagger

#9 Wreck the Halls

#10 Glitch and Famous (coming soon)

Raven Remington

Relentless 1

Relentless 2 (coming soon)

Holly Anna Paladin Mysteries:

#1 Random Acts of Murder

#2 Random Acts of Deceit

#2.5 Random Acts of Scrooge

#3 Random Acts of Malice

#4 Random Acts of Greed

#5 Random Acts of Fraud

#6 Random Acts of Outrage

#7 Random Acts of Iniquity

Lantern Beach Mysteries

#1 Hidden Currents

#2 Flood Watch

#3 Storm Surge

#4 Dangerous Waters

#5 Perilous Riptide

#6 Deadly Undertow

Lantern Beach Romantic Suspense

Tides of Deception

Shadow of Intrigue

Storm of Doubt

Winds of Danger

Lantern Beach P.D.

On the Lookout

Attempt to Locate

First Degree Murder

Dead on Arrival

Plan of Action

Lantern Beach Escape

Afterglow (a novelette)

Lantern Beach Blackout

coming soon

Carolina Moon Series

Home Before Dark

Gone By Dark

Wait Until Dark

Light the Dark

Taken By Dark

Suburban Sleuth Mysteries:

Death of the Couch Potato's Wife

Fog Lake Suspense:

Edge of Peril

Margin of Error

Brink of Danger

Line of Duty

Cape Thomas Series:

Dubiosity

Disillusioned

Distorted

Standalone Romantic Mystery:

The Good Girl

Suspense:

Imperfect

The Wrecking

Sweet Christmas Novella:

Home to Chestnut Grove

Standalone Romantic-Suspense:

Keeping Guard

The Last Target

Race Against Time

Ricochet

Key Witness

Lifeline

High-Stakes Holiday Reunion

Desperate Measures

Hidden Agenda

Mountain Hideaway

Dark Harbor

Shadow of Suspicion

The Baby Assignment

The Cradle Conspiracy

Trained to Defend

Nonfiction:

Characters in the Kitchen

Changed: True Stories of Finding God through Christian Music (out of print)

The Novel in Me: The Beginner's Guide to Writing and Publishing a Novel (out of print)

CHAPTER ONE

AS I AMBLED between the trees on the mountainside, nature parted at my entrance and practically rolled out a red carpet.

My psychologist had once told me I had delusions of grandeur.

He didn't know what he was talking about. He simply couldn't see what I could. He didn't know my importance.

Not yet.

"Abigail!" I called, making sure my voice was singsongy. "Or maybe I should call you Abi-*fail*? Abi-*jail*?"

Abi-jail. I liked that. This woman should be in prison. Instead, I'd serve her my own kind of justice.

The woman looked back at me, her dark hair flying out in a circle around her head. The action only intensified the look of terror in her eyes. It was like every part of her body knew the danger she was in and tried to flee in desperation.

She released a muffled cry and continued sprinting through the skeletal forest. The girl was an accident waiting to happen, running like that on this steep, rocky mountain. She couldn't be familiar with the terrain. No, she'd always been an inside girl.

I made a clucking sound with my tongue. Some people had to learn these lessons the hard way. Abi-jail had a long list of lessons she needed to learn.

I was going to teach her as many as I could. Unfortunately, some of the lessons would be painful . . . and ultimately deadly.

I began whistling my favorite song, "Little Red Riding Hood" by Sam the Sham and the Pharaohs. I liked thinking of myself as the Big Bad Wolf. Except, in my story, I'd be the one with the happy ending.

Abi-jail cried out and ran faster. Her arms flailed beside her. Any time now, she was going to trip. I just needed to be patient.

Nature continued to make a way for me as I paced through the pine and oak forest. The whole world was on my side, welcoming me to do the task it couldn't—to bring justice to the guilty. Not a namby-pamby kind of justice the US legal system tried to use. I preferred a more primal type. I practically drooled at the thought of it.

As the ground sloped, I took note of the leaves beneath my feet. They were slick and thick, hiding rocks beneath them, and reminding me of what was so wrong with this world today. This planet was full of morons who tried to sugarcoat the danger of a dark world littered with the trappings of the flesh.

My whistling faded.

Abi-jail still sprinted away from me. I knew she saw me. Occasionally, she cried out and fear invaded the sound, strangling it.

Pleasure curled through me. She should be scared.

She hadn't expected to see me. Not yet. Truth be told, it had taken me a long time to track her down in her hiding place. All the stars had aligned for me to find her, just as the path cleared for me to chase her now.

I didn't bother to quicken my steps. I'd take my time. Delight filled me every time I saw how frightened she was. I began to whistle again . . .

Soon, this would all be over.

My smile widened, and a burst of bliss shot through me.

I would be Abby's judge, jury . . . and executioner.

And it was going to be so much fun.

CHAPTER TWO

ABBY BRENNAN GLANCED over her shoulder, panic racing through her.

He was still there. Still following her.

"No!" The word escaped before she could stop it.

How had this man found her?

She had no idea. But she couldn't let him catch her. Her life depended on it.

Please, Lord . . . she lifted the silent prayer as dry branches scraped her arms. As rocks cut into her feet. As fear tightened her lungs.

"Abigail," he taunted, his deep, calm voice carrying through the air. "Abi-fail. Abi-jail."

The sick feeling in her gut bubbled up until she thought she might hurl.

Why couldn't he leave her alone? Why couldn't he realize her guilt was enough punishment? She didn't need to be on this vigilante's Most Wanted list.

Abby gasped as another rock cut her foot. She wanted to stop. Wanted to check her skin for any blood or visible injury.

But she couldn't afford that luxury. She had to get as far away from him as possible. Every second counted.

She nearly limped now. Was she leaving a trail of blood for him to follow?

Another cry lodged in her throat, the sound offset by the man's creepy whistle. What was that song? Why did it sound so haunting?

The man seemed too happy, like a psychopath who got pleasure—and strength—from other people's fear. He moved so calmly behind her, almost as if he knew what the outcome of the situation would be.

All Abby could see was his blue hat, pulled down low. A blue jacket. White skin. A salt-and-pepper-colored beard.

Her heart thumped into her chest as he continued to whistle.

"Abby . . ." He drew out the word.

She heard the leaves being crushed under his weight. Heard the branches snapping in obedience. Even the birds had quieted, almost as if they were terrified also.

How would Abby ever outrun him? How could she escape? Even worse—what if she couldn't?

Another cry escaped from her at the thought.

She glanced back at him once more, desperate to see how close he was.

As she did, the ground disappeared beneath her.

And she was falling . . . falling . . .

Then a terrible pain ripped through her, and everything went black.

ABBY JERKED HER EYES OPEN. As scorching sunlight burned into her pupils, she pressed them shut again. A cold wind swept over her skin, and she moaned.

At once, everything rushed back to her.

The man had found her.

Her hideout had been discovered.

But how?

With a jerk, she sat up. Pain ripped through her

skull. Abby reached for the spot on the back of her head. When she pulled her hand in front of her, she saw blood.

Red stained her fingers, congealed in her hair. Her head wobbled at the thought, and consciousness threatened to slip away again. She couldn't let that happen.

Snippets of her terror replayed in her mind.

That was right. She'd been running when suddenly the ground had disappeared beneath her. It wasn't exactly a cliff, but the drop was steep, probably twenty or thirty feet.

She'd landed here and must've hit her head.

She swung her gaze around as panic snaked around her lungs. Was the Executioner still here? Was he watching her? Waiting to finish the job? He'd been sending her threats for months.

Not just any threats either. They were detailed notes about how he would like to make her pay. Details had included mutilation, torture . . . and finally—mercifully—death.

Abby's lungs tightened more until she could hardly breathe. Her head continued to pound, to pound, and pound, pound, pound.

She scanned her surroundings. Mountains trapped her like a razor-topped fence. A trickling river whispered secrets a few feet away. Rocky boulders scattered the area, as if nature had decided to stone the landscape as punishment and leave the remnants of the horrible act behind.

Abby saw no one, but that didn't mean the man wasn't nearby. That he wasn't watching and planning her demise.

How had he even found her here? She'd been so secluded.

It didn't matter. All that mattered right now was surviving. If the Executioner didn't kill her, this wilderness would. Abby was miles from any civilization. She didn't even know which direction to head in order to get back to her cabin, to her car. What was she going to do?

Hold yourself together, Abby. That's the most important thing you can do right now.

Her dad had taught her some basic survival skills, and right now Abby wished she'd paid more attention.

She needed to get moving. The temperature in this area would drop into the twenties this evening. All she was wearing was a flannel shirt and jeans. She hadn't planned on running when she did, or she would've grabbed a jacket, hat, and shoes. But fleeing for your life didn't come with a five-minute warning.

As she shifted to stand, more pain shot through her skull. Her hip ached as she forced her body upright. Her shoulder felt sore and tender.

She was going to feel like death tomorrow. To say the least.

If she survived until tomorrow.

Her heartbeat quickened.

"Please, God," she whispered. "Help me."

Pushing aside her pain, Abby glanced around. If she followed the stream, would it eventually lead to civilization?

She knew that the tourist town of Fog Lake, Tennessee, was about fifteen miles from the cabin where she'd been staying. The river probably flowed into the lake, right? The logic made sense to her.

Abby shivered. The wilderness had seemed so tranquil and serene at one time. Now, the area seemed like a graveyard and each of the barren trees tombstones.

Just move, Abby. She couldn't waste any time. If Fog Lake was fifteen miles away, it was going to take her a good portion of the day to walk there. And that was provided that this path was even passable. She prayed her injury didn't slow her down.

Her heart pounded.

She could do this. She could find help. Then she'd decide her next step in handling this situation.

But as Abby stared at nature all around her, despair tried to bite deep. Right now, the miles of desolation felt more like solitary confinement.

CHAPTER THREE

"SO JAXON, YOU CATCHING ANYTHING YET?"

Jaxon glanced over at his brother Boone and gave him a dirty look when he saw the smug expression on his face. "No luck yet. Stop bragging."

"I'm just saying . . . if this was a competition—which it isn't—but if it was, I'd totally be winning right now." Boone flashed him a rakish grin.

Jaxon had missed his brothers and sister. But he'd be lying if he said that coming back to Fog Lake had been easy. No, *leaving* had been the easy part. Coming home was like trying to return to the past, only to find everything had changed.

That familiar tension pulled across his chest.

He reeled his line in, knowing there was nothing on the other end except maybe some bait.

He and his brothers had gone away for a weekend camping trip. It wasn't the most ideal time to go camping. Not in Fog Lake in February. But the Wilder brothers had been taught all things outdoors by their father, who had passed away a few years ago.

Jaxon knew his brothers had hoped this trip might bond them. They probably hoped that he might open up about the real reasons he'd returned home from the military. But he still wasn't ready.

Jaxon put his fishing pole down. "I think I'm going to take a breather and go for a walk."

"You need company?" His oldest brother, Luke, set his fishing pole on one of the huge rocks lining the river. He looked so relaxed as he lounged back in his camping chair, staring at the water. The man needed to relax. As sheriff in Fog Lake, his job had been surprisingly busy lately.

"Nah." Jaxon took a step away and breathed in a long, slow breath of fresh mountain air. "I think I could use some time by myself."

He didn't miss the look his brothers exchanged. They were worried about him. Jaxon couldn't blame them.

He'd returned home from deployment a different person than he'd been when he left. The things he experienced while in the Middle East had been a wakeup call. In some ways, he was still learning to live with himself. He'd once been social. Now he felt like a loner. He used to trust people. Now he trusted no one.

As he meandered along the riverbank, he climbed to the top of a boulder, scanned the river, and drew in a deep breath. He'd either find himself here or lose himself completely.

He was about to hop down when something farther up the river caught his eye.

Was that a person?

Jaxon narrowed his gaze, trying to figure out what it was he was seeing.

That definitely looked like a person. But he and his brothers were miles away from anything. Who else would be out here?

It didn't matter. Maybe somebody else had escaped into the national forest to get some privacy, and Jaxon should leave them alone.

He started to turn away, but something stopped him. Something instinctual.

What if it wasn't a person who'd come out here for privacy? What if it was someone who needed help?

Jaxon didn't know the answer to that. The only

way he would know was if he got closer. What could it hurt?

He jumped off the boulder and started across the stones, trying to keep his boots dry. The closer he got to the person, the more his worry grew.

The stranger appeared to be kneeling and holding their head.

No, make that *her* head.

Based on the long, dark hair and slim build, that looked like a woman out here alone.

Carefully, Jaxon continued to maneuver around the rocky river. He was getting closer now. He could clearly see a woman bent over as if in pain.

He sucked in breath. Was that blood on the back of her head?

He was nearly certain it was.

He quickened his steps, now desperate to know if she was okay. She was clearly in trouble. "Ma'am, can I help you?"

The woman glanced up, the look on her face reminding him of someone who'd been sucker punched. Her eyes were red with desperation. Her skin pale with pain. Her limbs shaky with shock.

Just as Jaxon reached her, she started to collapse. Jaxon caught her before she hit the rocks.

"Ma'am?"

Desperate eyes met his. With surprising strength, she grasped his arms, demanding his attention. "Please . . . don't let him . . . find me . . ."

The next instant, she buckled in his arms.

JAXON PACED the hall at the hospital, unable to get the woman out of his mind. She'd been in with the doctors for the past two hours. Boone and Luke were here also, Luke waiting to take her statement as soon as the doctor cleared her.

What had happened to her? Her words haunted Jaxon.

Please don't let him find me.

It almost felt as if God had handed him a second chance to make things right.

After Jaxon had found her, he'd taken the woman back to his brothers, and they'd called an emergency helicopter to come for a rescue operation. There was no other way to get her out of the remote location in her weakened state. Jaxon and his brothers had been too far away from help.

Luke leaned against the wall in the hallway, still dressed in camping attire, though he was officially on duty as of now. The waiting room was full, so they lingered here instead. A nurse had brought them a couple folding chairs.

Jaxon watched as Luke turned to him. His oldest brother had a tall, lean frame and chiseled features. His hair was dark and cut away from his face. He was traditional. A leader. Always dependable.

Those qualities had always defined Luke.

He'd been busy doing some paperwork and talking to the rescue crew. "So what did she say again?"

"She said, 'Please don't let him find me,'" Jaxon repeated, tension snaking down his spine as he remembered the woman's desperate words.

"It sounds like she was running from someone." Boone crossed his arms.

Boone was the middle brother. Slightly rebellious, with lighter hair that curled at the ends and was always a little too long. He was an outdoorsman who loved adventure. Right now, he wore his baseball cap backward, and the sleeves of his flannel shirt were rolled up his forearms.

"I didn't see anyone else out there," Luke said. "Did you?"

Jaxon shook his head. He'd mentally reviewed the scene more than once. "I didn't see anyone all weekend. I have no idea where she came from. Then again, she obviously has a head injury, so maybe she's delusional."

"I guess we'll find out when I talk to her." As soon as Luke said the words, the door opened and a stout, gray-haired doctor stepped out.

Dr. Keagan, his jacket read. His gaze went right to Luke. "Ms. Michaels is still weak and a little confused, but she said she'd talk to you."

"So she's okay?" Luke asked, snapping into professional mode.

"All things considered, she's doing pretty well. She has a mild concussion, as well as a few cuts and bruises. It's a near miracle she didn't break any bones." Dr. Keagan nodded behind him. "Go on in and talk to her yourself."

As Luke disappeared into the room, Jaxon sat down in one of the chairs that had been left against the hallway wall.

"That was some camping trip," Boone muttered.

"You can say that again. Things are never boring when the Wilder brothers are around."

Boone chuckled. "No, they're not. We did manage to light the biggest bonfire this town had ever seen."

"If dad hadn't been sheriff, we would have probably been arrested."

"We did get six months of community service."

Jaxon smiled before glancing down the hallway. A shadow there caused him to bristle. It almost seemed like someone had been watching around the corner and then ducked to avoid being caught.

"Jaxon?" Boone asked.

Jaxon barely heard him. Something about that figure bothered him, beckoned his attention. "Excuse me a minute."

Before anyone could stop him, Jaxon took off toward the movement. Given what had just happened, he wasn't going to take any chances.

CHAPTER FOUR

JAXON RUSHED DOWN THE HALLWAY. Where had that person gone?

He hadn't been imagining things. Someone had been there. His gut told him it was someone who was up to no good.

He darted around the corner, but this corridor was empty also—except for the stairway door that clicked shut at the end of the hallway.

Picking up his pace, Jaxon jogged toward it.

He reached for his waist, where he'd normally kept his gun. But he didn't have it with him now. If there was a predator lurking in this hospital, he was going to have to face him unarmed.

He fisted his hands at the thought.

He reached the stairway and stepped inside cautiously.

No one was within eyesight.

He paused. Listened.

Nothing.

Then a slam.

Someone had just exited below him.

He rushed down the steps until he reached the first floor. As he stepped through the doorway, he saw swarms of people walking the hall there.

What . . . ?

It was a choir, he realized. They must be arriving to sing in the lobby. Sometimes this hospital brought in guests from the community to do things like that. He'd heard some nurses talking about it earlier.

Jaxon stepped through the crowd, still looking for the shadow.

But it was too late. The man was gone. Jaxon would never be able to figure out who he was in this crowd.

But he would be keeping his eyes open in the future.

Who was the guy? Why had he been here?

Had someone been chasing that woman through the woods? A picture began forming in Jaxon's head.

A picture of someone doing just that. Following

the woman. Then realizing she wasn't dead and coming here to the hospital to finish her off.

Was Jaxon reading too much into this?

He didn't know.

But he didn't like the theories that lingered in his mind.

He hurried back upstairs and sat down beside his brother.

"Everything okay?" Boone's eyes narrowed with confusion.

Jaxon nodded. "Yeah, I thought I saw someone I knew. Must have slipped away before I could catch him."

Boone's gaze remained narrowed, as if he didn't believe him.

Before he could press Jaxon anymore, Luke stepped from the woman's room. His face looked serious and tight along with his shoulders.

Jaxon stood, anxious to hear an update. "Well?"

Luke paused in front of him and let out a breath. "She claims she just got lost in the woods."

Jaxon wasn't buying that. "What about her head injury?"

"She said she walked too close to a cliff and accidentally fell." Luke rubbed his jaw. "But she didn't mention anything strange was going on. Just that she was here for a personal retreat until the end of the week, maybe longer."

Something about the story didn't ring true for Jaxon. He'd seen the woman's eyes and heard her voice. He knew there was more to this story. But what?

Luke's radio beeped. He stepped away, muttered a few things into it before striding back toward them.

"There's been an accident on Main Street. I need to get down there. My deputies are tied up right now with a domestic situation." He frowned as he looked at Abby's room, as if trying to figure out what to do with her.

Boone glanced at his watch. "I'd stay, but I told Brynlee I'd be home for dinner tonight. I'm sure if I call her, she'll understand."

Luke's jaw flexed. "The doctor said Ms. Michaels would be cleared to go in about an hour. By then, one of my guys should be free to give her a ride."

"I'll drive her back to her place," Jaxon offered.

His brothers turned to him, surprise written in their wide eyes. Jaxon wasn't sure why they were treating him as if he were a stranger or fragile. There were clearly unspoken conversations between them.

"Are you sure?" Luke finally asked.

Jaxon shrugged. "I don't mind. I don't have anything else to do."

Luke stared at him uncertainly for one more second before finally nodding. "If you're okay with it, then I'm okay with it. Of course, Abby has to agree also."

Abby . . . that seemed a fitting name for the woman. She looked like an Abby with her long, dark hair, her tanned skin, and her petite build.

"My truck is just down the street where I left it before the camping trip," Jaxon said. "How about if I go grab it and bring it here? That way, I can take her back as soon as she's ready."

Luke clasped his shoulder. "Thanks, man. I appreciate it. If you need anything else, let me know."

Jaxon didn't tell him, but he had ulterior motives for wanting to stay. He wanted to look this woman in the eyes and find out what was really going on. He couldn't press it, but he felt certain that this woman was in danger.

ABBY SHIVERED. She hadn't stopped shivering since she'd arrived at the hospital and regained consciousness. The flimsy sheet over her legs did nothing to help her.

She rubbed her head, feeling the ache there. The stitches. The familiar feeling of hopelessness echoed with every throb.

The Executioner had found her. The man actually called himself the Judge, Jury, and Executioner in the threats he sent her. Abby thought Executioner said enough.

Nausea gurgled in her stomach at the thought.

The police back home hadn't been able to pinpoint who he was. They'd been hardly any help, probably in light of the media circus around her life. But Abby had known the man's threats were real.

Abby had seen the man watching her. She'd felt his presence, even when no one else had seen him. He was the one who'd dug up dirt on her, who'd fed reporters even more lies in an effort to ruin her.

Right now, with little money and resources, running was a near impossibility. A new wave of anxiety rushed over her. How would she escape from this man?

A soft knock sounded at the door. She called, "Come in," and a man stepped inside.

It took Abby a moment to realize who he was.

This was the man who'd rescued her. How could she forget?

He appeared to be in his mid-twenties, with a squarish face and dark hair that was cut short. Something about him seemed mysterious, strong, and silent.

He shoved his hands into his jeans pockets and stepped forward. "I'm Jaxon. Jaxon Wilder."

"I'm Abby." Her voice came out shakier than she wanted. "Thank you for your help earlier, and I'm sorry I had to put you through that. I heard you were out camping when you found me."

"And I heard that you were out hiking." He paused. "Barefooted."

Warmth flooded her cheeks, and she looked down at her lap. She'd made up the story on the fly. If she'd told the sheriff what was really going on, he would've asked too many questions. People might find out who she was, and Abby couldn't risk that.

"I know it seems flighty," she said. "I should've known better. But I didn't intend on being out long. It seemed like such a simple little walk until I finally realized that I had no idea where I was."

Jaxon nodded slowly, almost as if he didn't believe her. "You're out this way by yourself then?"

The man was certainly asking a lot of questions.

He wasn't law enforcement—apparently, his brother held that position. Yet Jaxon seemed equally as inquisitive.

Abby wanted to shoo him away, to tell him it wasn't his business. It *wasn't* his business, but the man had saved her life, so she didn't want to be nasty.

Thankfully, just then, the doctor came in with her discharge papers.

"You're free to go," he announced.

Surprise rippled through her. "Already? That's . . . great."

"Make sure you rest, avoid too much activity for the next twenty-four hours, and limit anything that triggers your symptoms," the doctor said. "Take acetaminophen and try to stay on top of the pain."

The next instant, Abby was on her feet. Thankfully, a nurse had come in earlier and helped to clean her up. Her head had been stitched, she'd been given some pain medication, and the hospital had found some new clothes for her to wear since hers were torn and wet.

She grabbed the bed railing to keep her balance. The questions swirling in her head—among other things—made her feel unsteady.

How was she going to get back to her cabin? Did she even want to go back there?

What if he was there?

She squeezed her eyes shut as fear did a wicked dance across her skin.

"I can give you a ride," Jaxon said, as if reading her mind.

Abby glanced at him again. The man seemed laid-back and unassuming. But was he? She was a terrible judge of character.

She licked her lips. "I hate to put you out. I've already messed up your schedule."

"We don't exactly have Uber around here. Maybe I should think about being the first driver that they hire." He shrugged, an almost boyish look about him.

Could Abby trust this man? The question seemed silly considering he'd just saved her life. Still, she didn't like relying on strangers for help. What other choice did she have, though?

Finally, she nodded. "If you don't mind, I'll take you up on that offer. But I promise I'll be out of your hair after that."

Jaxon would drop her off, Abby would hop in her car, and she'd start to drive. She'd keep going for as long as she could, trying to outrun the Executioner. She saw no other options.

"It's no problem." He reached for her arm, helping her toward the wheelchair the nurse had brought in.

Abby wanted to argue, to say she didn't need it. But then she would only make a bigger spectacle of herself. She'd come here because she hadn't wanted to be seen. She needed to do whatever possible to keep a low profile now.

With a frown, she sat down. She desperately needed to recalculate.

But the biggest question in her mind was about the Executioner. Did he think Abby was dead? Or would he come back to finish what he started?

Her trembles started all over again.

As the nurse pushed Abby into the hallway, Abby's gaze swerved to the left, then the right. She waited, expecting to see him again.

She saw no one.

But that didn't mean he wasn't close.

CHAPTER FIVE

JAXON GRIPPED his steering wheel as he headed farther and farther into the heart of the mountains. Wherever Abby's cabin was, it was isolated. Usually women coming to Fog Lake by themselves didn't pick places so remote. They chose little cabins down by the lake or the hotel near the downtown area.

Questions continued to stir in his mind about the woman beside him. What was she hiding? Why had she looked so scared the moment she left that hospital room?

Right now, she sat quietly in his truck, staring out the window. She had a prescription bottle in one hand and instructions from the doctor in the other.

Who would help her tonight? Who would make sure nothing happened to her in her current state?

After a head injury like that, she shouldn't be left alone.

It wasn't Jaxon's business or concern. Yet Jaxon felt uneasy about the whole situation. The woman had secrets. She was scared. And, apparently, she was all alone.

Put that all together, and it equaled trouble.

"What brings you to this area?" Jaxon finally asked, trying to make small talk. He'd never been very good at it.

As soon as the question left his lips, Abby squirmed and glanced at him. As quickly as her tell-tale nerves had appeared, they vanished again. "I like to do personal retreats once a year. This area seemed just as good as any."

Her answer sounded rehearsed. He'd questioned terrorists before. He should know when a person was lying, and Abby was trying to sell him a big, fat one right now.

"A personal retreat sounds nice. Where are you from?"

"Michigan," she said. "The Upper Peninsula."

"I didn't peg your accent for up there." Jaxon's roommate had been from Muskegon. He'd never called it the Upper Peninsula. It was always the U.P., and he'd always demonstrated where it was by using his hand as a mitten. He'd said it was a Michigan thing.

"I grew up all over, so I don't really have an accent," she said. "At least, that's what people tell me."

"I'm surprised there weren't any places closer to home where you'd want to go for a retreat." Jaxon knew he was pushing, but he wanted answers. He couldn't help her unless he had answers, even though the woman hadn't asked for his assistance. She probably wouldn't even accept his help if he offered. That didn't stop him.

"There's just something about the Smoky Mountains that puts my mind at ease. What can I say?" The words came out lighthearted, and the shrug Abby offered seemed to match.

But Jaxon still wasn't buying it.

"I can understand that. What is it that you do for a living?" That was small talk, right? Why did it feel like an interrogation? Jaxon tried to keep his tone light, even though he knew he was failing.

"I work in a restaurant." She rubbed her hands across her jeans. "It doesn't pay great, but I really like it."

Her voice softened some, as if she were relieved that she didn't have to lie again.

"I see." He wanted to ask more, but he stopped himself.

Abby cleared her throat and glanced at him. Or had that been a twitch? "Enough about me, how about you? Let me guess, military?"

Jaxon's grip tightened on the steering wheel. "How did you know?"

"You can always tell the military guys. They carry themselves differently."

Jaxon couldn't argue with her. She must have lived around the military to know that. There weren't many bases on the Upper Peninsula, though. Not to his knowledge, at least. "I just got out of the Army."

"And why did you come here?"

He noted how she turned the tables on him. Maybe she needed a break from his questions. It was only fair. "My family is here, so I came back so I could reconnect."

"Sounds like a smart idea."

He didn't know how smart it was. To his brothers, Jaxon would always be the little brother who left home. The little brother who wasn't capable of making decisions but who needed to be coddled.

Jaxon had enjoyed his time away. He'd been able to be his own person. He'd led a group of men who'd looked up to him. It was quite the change from his home life.

He was beginning to see why his questions had made Abby uncomfortable. Maybe he should have stuck to talking about the weather or sports.

"Turn here." Abby pointed to a gravel lane up ahead.

Jaxon did as she said. The road narrowed as they continued to climb upward. The engine roared into lower gear. Gravel kicked out beneath the tires. The trees moved in closer.

"How did you ever find this place?" Jaxon glanced around, realizing this wasn't the kind of location where you wanted to break down or get lost —and he was from this area. "It's one of the more secluded cabins around here, and I've been to a lot of them. When I was in high school, I used to work in maintenance for one of the rental agencies in Fog Lake."

"Is that right?" A quiver rattled Abby's words, and she cleared her throat. "I don't know what to say. I was looking online and came across this place and thought it would be perfect. What can I say? Advertising works."

"I see."

"Turn here." She directed him up a dirt path that splintered from the gravel road.

The closer they got to her house, the more Jaxon sensed her nerves. It seemed as though Abby tried to conceal them, but it was evident, almost like her body was giving off a telltale vibe.

A moment later, they pulled to a stop in front of a small cabin surrounded by nothing but woods. Miles and miles of woods.

"Here we are." Abby's skin looked even paler than it had before as she stared at the place.

Her reaction only confirmed that she was terrified. Jaxon knew he needed to help, but he needed to figure out how.

"Do you mind if I walk you up?" He softened his voice, trying not to scare her off.

After a moment of silence, Abby nodded. "Sure. Just . . . be careful."

"Be careful?" What did she mean by that?

She shrugged. "I mean, there are bears around here and everything. You know . . ."

Jaxon knew only that this woman was in trouble, and that thought made his stomach churn as memories of Iraq tried to pummel him.

~

ABBY ATTEMPTED to hide the tremor that claimed her muscles again. It had been there, almost dormant during the drive. But it was definitely still there, still present and trying to claw to the surface.

As she reached for the door handle, her shaking became more uncontrollable. Abby pulled her hand back into her lap before Jaxon could see it. He seemed observant. He'd probably already noticed.

She stepped out of the truck, her lungs tight. What if he was here? The Executioner?

Abby glanced around. The sun had begun to sink lower now. A lone bird seemed to squawk a warning. Dry leaves scraped against the ground like a killer dragging his weapon.

She flinched, her mind drifting back to earlier today.

Earlier to when she'd been reading on the couch, drinking coffee, and had glanced out the window.

The action had been casual, without any real reason except to look at the mountains.

The Executioner had stood there. Somehow, she'd instinctively known it was him.

He stared at the cabin, almost as if he were waiting for her to appear in that very window.

Abby had nearly passed out.

Then she'd done the only thing she knew to do

—she'd taken off out the back door. He hadn't even chased her. He didn't need to.

Because Abby knew what that man would do to her if he caught her.

"Abby?"

She let out a half-gasp, half-scream. As her thoughts came back to the present, she saw Jaxon standing there. He stared at her as if she'd lost her mind.

He touched her elbow. Part of Abby wanted to shoo him away, but she was thankful for his help— even if his touch did send a tingle down her spine.

Tingles down her spine had always gotten her in trouble, and she had no desire to take it any further. Dating, romance, men—they were all a mistake she'd never make again. She was better off being alone, even if being alone felt like a miserable way to live.

"You okay?" Jaxon peered at her, seeming to see right through her façade and into the depths of her soul.

The realization was unnerving, to say the least. The more closed off she was, the better. Self-preservation had to take center stage.

"Of course, of course. I'm fine. Just trying to get my footing again after everything that happened."

She touched her head, reaching for the spot she'd hit when she fell. It throbbed again, though she wondered if the headache was more situational than physical. Either way, it hurt.

Jaxon didn't say anything, but something about the look in his eyes indicated he didn't believe her. Abby remained silent, not wanting to give up any more than necessary. Carefully, Jaxon helped her to the steps of her cabin.

She froze on the porch. Her door was cracked open. She hadn't left it like that. Not the front door. She'd kept this place locked up tight, and she'd fled out the back door.

"Wait here." Jaxon bristled, his muscles tightening as his broad chest blocked her from the doorway. "Let me make sure everything is clear inside."

It was almost as if Jaxon knew she was in danger. But that was impossible, right? He didn't know who she really was.

She'd told people she'd gone on a hike and had gotten lost. She hadn't said anything to him when he'd rescued her ... right? It was all a blur.

Even as Abby tried to reassure herself, her head began to pound again. This time, she knew for a fact it wasn't from her injury but from her lies.

Jaxon slipped inside.

She'd never wanted to live with pretenses like this. But Abby had been left with no other choice. She didn't know what else she could do right now, and she hoped people might forgive her if they found out the startling truth.

Everything quieted around her. The squawking bird even went silent. Did it know something she didn't?

Her lungs filled with cement again, and she glanced around.

Was the Executioner here? Was he watching?

Or what if he was inside with Jaxon? What if something had happened to the Good Samaritan who'd rescued her?

Please, God . . . protect him. And, if I'm not asking too much, please protect me too. A whimper escaped from her lips as the events leading up to this moment pummeled her. *I didn't know . . . if I had, I would have done things differently back in Georgia.*

Georgia . . . where she was really from. Where she owned a bakery. Where people knew her as Abby Brennan.

She glanced at the door, feeling a panic attack coming on. She couldn't breathe. Her muscles trembled so badly they nearly vibrated. Her eyes couldn't stop darting around.

She shouldn't have come back here.

But it was too late now.

What if the Executioner had hurt Jaxon? Maybe Abby needed to go check on him. So why did she feel rooted to this spot, like she was a statue unable to move?

A footfall sounded beside her. A gargled scream escaped from her lips as she twirled, ready to run again.

"It's just me," Jaxon murmured. He started to reach for her but dropped his hand.

Abby nodded, probably too quickly. Her heart still raced out of control.

It was Jaxon. He was okay. He was alive.

And, for just a moment at least, Abby felt safe again.

"Sorry. I'm jumpy."

"Falls can do that to a person." Was he being sincere? Did he suspect there was more to her story?

"It looks clear inside." He shifted, hesitated a moment, and then shook his head. "But I'm not comfortable leaving you here."

Leaving her here? The thought caused spikes of fear to shoot up her spine. She had no one to depend on right now but herself.

"I'm sure I'll be fine." Abby could barely croak out the words.

Jaxon leaned closer, his studious eyes watching her every expression. "How are you going to get help if you need it? You probably don't even have cell phone service out here, do you?"

"I actually didn't even bring a phone with me." Abby didn't tell him the real reason behind that. She didn't want to be traced and couldn't take any chances. It hadn't done any good, though. The Executioner had found her anyway.

Jaxon raised his eyebrows and nodded. "Okay, so no phone. What about your car?"

"What about my car?" Abby wondered what Jaxon was getting at. He should clearly be able to see it in the driveway beside the house.

He nodded toward the sedan. "You have two flat tires."

"What?" Abby's gaze swerved toward the vehicle.

He was right.

Her tires were deflated and uneven.

A hollow feeling formed in her stomach, followed by a surge of panic.

The Executioner had known she was going to come back, hadn't he?

He'd anticipated it. Why would he do that? What would it prove?

The skin on her neck rose, and she glanced around.

He'd done it to trap her here with no means of escape.

He wanted to finish what he started.

In fact, he was probably hiding in those woods now, watching her and waiting for an opportunity to make his next move.

CHAPTER SIX

JAXON WATCHED as Abby's face turned even paler. Her eyes twitched, and tremors claimed her limbs again.

He stiffened, sensing she was on the verge of panic.

He'd planned on checking her tires to see what had happened to them, but he couldn't leave her in this state, even to go a few steps away. He had no doubt her car had been sabotaged.

Abby stepped back, her gaze swerving around them. Her breaths came fast and furious, and Jaxon could sense the fear radiating from her body. She only stopped backing up when her legs hit the steps behind her, nearly toppling her.

"Abby?" The hair on Jaxon's neck rose as he

watched her—as more memories battered him. He desperately wanted to forget his failures, but the memories kept flashing back and putting him in his place.

Her wide eyes met his. "We've got to get out of here."

"Okay . . ." He still wasn't sure what set her off. He didn't see anything dangerous around them. "Do you want to grab anything?"

"No. We need to leave now. Please." Desperation cracked her voice. Abby continued to look around, as if she expected someone to emerge from the woods wielding a knife or gun.

He had no idea if the danger was real or imagined, but, for Abby's mental health, he wouldn't stick around to find out. She could worry about her belongings later.

"Let's go." Jaxon led her to his truck and tucked her inside. Her eyes continued to dart around and her limbs trembled uncontrollably.

He cranked the engine and pulled away from the property. Abby's shoulders remained tense until the cabin disappeared from sight. Even then, she remained uptight—just not quite as neurotic.

Jaxon didn't ask questions. Not yet. But he was a little more than curious.

The woman obviously couldn't stay at her cabin. She had no phone. No car. Probably no money.

Jaxon would take her to a hotel, but he knew they were all booked this week with two different corporate outings in town. He could take her to stay with one of his family members, but doing so would put either Ansley, Harper, or Brynlee in danger.

He didn't want to risk that.

Jaxon drove silently, giving Abby some space until they reached a parking lot near the town's namesake—Fog Lake. He pulled in at a spot facing the water and put his truck in Park. Heat blew through the vents, warming them and offering the steady noise of air flow.

He turned to Abby. "I want to help you, but first you need to tell me what's going on."

She stared out the front window, her breathing entirely too shallow.

Jaxon waited. He had all the time in the world. He didn't have a family to rush home to. He was out of the military now and working odd jobs until he figured out his future.

The sun was almost about to disappear on the picturesque horizon. What a day this had turned out to be.

He remained silent. Enough time passed that

Jaxon wondered if Abby would say anything at all. What was running through that head of hers?

"Someone's trying to kill me." Abby rubbed her throat, almost as if it hurt to say the words.

"Who?"

She quickly shrugged before shaking her head equally as quickly. "I don't know."

Jaxon stared at her, waiting for more. He didn't want to interrogate her. He preferred that she shared on her own.

But would she?

Still nothing.

She rubbed her hands on her jeans. Finally, she opened her door and . . . hurled.

Jaxon grabbed a tissue from the compartment beside him and handed it to her. She closed the door, shutting out the cool breeze before wiping her mouth and whispering, "Thank you."

He wished he had more to offer her—some water maybe—but he had nothing.

"Is there anything else you can tell me?"

Her hand remained at her throat, as if she might get sick again. "I don't know anything else. I started receiving threats a couple months ago. Noticed someone following me. Realized someone had been in my home. That's when I ran. I knew I had to get away. I came here, hoping this guy would leave me alone. I was wrong."

Jaxon's heart pounded in his ears. Her ordeal sounded horrific and justified her strong reaction. "We need to tell Luke—Sheriff Wilder."

"No!" Abby turned to him, her eyes wide. "I don't want to bring the police into this. I just want to disappear."

"How will that help anything? The police can protect you—"

"You don't understand . . ." She forcefully shook her head.

"Explain it to me then." Jaxon kept his voice calm.

She stared out the window and sucked in shaky breaths. Occasionally, something that sounded close to a whimper seemed to rumble in her chest. "Can we keep this just between us? Please?"

Jaxon knew the woman didn't owe him anything. But he really wanted more details. Could he keep Abby's secret? Yes. Would he? If he promised, then he'd have no other choice.

Finally, he let out a breath. "I suppose I can do that."

"Thank you."

"Is there anyone you can call?"

"No." She said the word so softly that Jaxon barely heard her. She reached for the door handle, as if she'd mentally changed gears. "I need to get out of your hair. I just—"

"I know a place where you can stay."

She froze. "I don't have much money."

"There's no cost."

She stared at him as if trying to get a read on the situation.

He shrugged. "I have an apartment above my place. You can stay there. No strings attached. It's clean and warm. You'll be safe."

"I couldn't possibly—"

"What other choice do you have?" Jaxon hated to remind her of the grim reality, but he felt it was his duty.

Abby remained quiet for a moment, her trembles dying down some. "None, I guess."

"I won't be far away. And you look like you could use some rest."

Abby's eyes appeared glazed, and she kept touching the back of her head. She wasn't in a good position to search for places to stay and ways to pay for it. Worry flooded through Jaxon.

He held his breath and waited for her response, praying she would let him help.

ABBY HATED to accept help from a stranger. But what choice did she have? She was at this man's mercy. Or perhaps it was grace that she'd found in him. She wasn't sure yet.

Maybe tomorrow she could go back to the cabin. Figure out a way to have her car fixed. Get her purse and her belongings.

She would find a solution. But, at least for tonight, she could take Jaxon up on his offer.

Abby glanced at the man beside her as they headed down the road. Part of her felt compelled—maybe even obligated—to share more than she had. But she couldn't.

If Jaxon knew the entire truth, he wouldn't want to help her. He would only judge her. That's what everyone else had done.

They'd formed conclusions without even asking her side of the story. Instead, they'd chosen the most sensational explanation, which left Abby painted as a villain.

As the miles blurred past, her eyes felt heavy. She was so, so tired.

She'd hardly slept the five days she'd been here. She hadn't been able to. Though logic had told her she was safe, fear constantly nudged her awake. She'd hoped for the best, but the worst had happened instead.

Finally, they came to a stop in front of a cabin located right on the lake. As Jaxon put the truck into Park, Abby stared up at the structure. The outside looked clean and neat, even in the dark. A moment of relief washed through her.

Abby prayed that she was doing the right thing and not putting herself in another bad situation. She had so few options right now, however.

She only hoped no one discovered who she really was. The revelation would bring a fire storm. In truth, Abby had come here not only to get away from the Executioner but to get away from the speculation.

How was it that she'd tried for her entire life to always do the right thing, and one decision had ruined all that? She'd hoped that her reputation could outshine any accusations, but that hadn't been the case. She felt like the most hated woman on the planet right now.

"Let's get you inside." Jaxon's voice broke her from her thoughts.

Abby nodded. "In case I haven't said this, thank

you. For everything. You've gone above and beyond. Most people would've run away by now."

"Well, I'm not most people."

She tried to smile. She wanted to. She really did.

Jaxon opened his door and hopped out, and she did the same. The air around her seemed even more frigid since the sun had set. A slight wind came off the lake, chilling everything in its path.

Jaxon lightly touched her back as he led her toward the front door. "I've been staying on the first floor since I bought this place, but the upstairs is fully furnished. The previous owner had a tenant."

"That sounds . . . perfect."

He pulled out his keys and unlocked the door, ushering her inside. "I'm going to let you stay down here where it's warm while I go upstairs and get things situated."

"I can help," she offered.

Jaxon waved her off. "No need for that. You've been through enough today."

She glanced around. The interior was surprisingly cozy, decorated like a typical mountain lodge. Yellow oak graced the floors, ceilings, and log walls. Brown leather furniture and plaid accents decorated the rest, and the vague aroma of coffee lingered in the air.

"Have a seat." Jaxon pointed at the couch.

Abby didn't argue. She was exhausted. So, so exhausted.

She watched as Jaxon went to the fireplace and started a blaze. The man had been a lifesaver. She couldn't stop reminding herself of that. Jaxon had come into her life at just the right moment, and she wasn't sure how she would ever thank him for what he had done.

"Make yourself comfortable." Jaxon stood from the fire. "There's water and food in the fridge. I'm going to head upstairs. Give me a few minutes to get things ready. I'll lock the door behind me. But, just to let you know, I was watching on the drive here. No one was behind us. No one should know where you are."

For now. That realization was all Abby could think of. She had no doubt she was living on borrowed time. Nothing she could do would change that.

As Jaxon left, she pulled the green plaid blanket from the back of the couch over her legs and settled into the cushions. The question was: would she get any sleep tonight?

CHAPTER SEVEN

FIFTEEN MINUTES LATER, Jaxon stepped back into his cabin and paused. Abby lay on his couch with a blanket around her shoulders and her eyes closed. He waited a moment to see if she'd stir.

Based on the steady rise and fall of her chest, she was asleep—and soundly, at that.

Quietly, he took a step, not wanting to disturb her. She probably needed the rest. He paused, his gaze lingering on her a moment.

Jaxon was more curious than ever as to what her story was. At least she'd opened up and shared that someone was trying to kill her. It was a start. But he had a feeling there were far more details she hadn't been forthcoming about.

Jaxon intended on keeping his promise not to tell

anyone what was going on with her, but there was no way he could avoid letting his brothers and sister know that this woman was staying here.

As he heard tires on the gravel outside, he stepped onto his porch. He watched as the approaching car cut the headlights. A moment later, his sister Ansley emerged from the driver seat with a paper bag in her hands.

"Hey, bro," she said, starting toward him.

He still couldn't get over the changes in his sister. When he had left Fog Lake, she'd been rebellious, with platinum-blonde hair, multiple earrings, and new tattoos every other month, it seemed. But she'd had some wakeup calls, and, since then, she'd really grown up.

Her hair was back to its natural dark-brown color. She gotten rid of some of her piercings, and her tattoos could no longer be seen due to the more modest clothing she wore. She was now dating his childhood best friend Ryan Philips, and Jaxon couldn't be happier for the two.

"Thanks for coming by." Jaxon took the bag from her outstretched arm and tucked it beside him.

They paused on the porch. Even though it was cold outside, the temperatures didn't bother him.

He'd always preferred winter to summer and found the cool air invigorating.

Ansley glanced through the window into his house, where the fireplace cast an orange glow. "What's going on?"

"You mean, you didn't hear?" Jaxon knew his brothers. No doubt they'd called Ansley to let her know what happened. Or, if they didn't tell her, no doubt his sisters-in-law had. That wasn't necessarily a bad thing. His family just liked to keep each other in the loop. It could be a blessing or a curse, depending on the situation.

"Yes, I did hear about all your adventures today. But what I didn't hear about was why this woman is at your place right now." Ansley gave him a pointed look.

Jaxon let out a long breath and remembered his promise to Abby. He chose his words carefully. "She needed a place to stay, and she's been through a lot. I was going to let her stay upstairs, but while I was getting things ready, she fell asleep on the couch."

Ansley glanced through the window again. "So you're just going to let her crash there?"

"She's sleeping so well that I hate to wake her."

Ansley shrugged, never one to act holier than thou. "I can't blame you. What's her story?"

"I don't know yet." Jaxon leaned against the rough side of the cabin. "I'm waiting for her to tell me on her terms."

Ansley glanced back inside, her gaze lingering this time. "She's pretty."

"That doesn't have anything to do with this."

"I didn't say it did." Ansley raised her hands in innocence. "It was just an observation. She looks . . . familiar."

"Maybe you saw her around town."

"Maybe."

His sister had barely been a teenager when Jaxon had decided to join the Army. He'd known he couldn't stay here any longer, but his sister had been the hardest part about saying goodbye.

"Anyway . . ." Ansley straightened. "I hope the clothes and other things I picked out will work."

She'd purchased a toothbrush and some other toiletries, just in case Abby needed them. Jaxon hadn't wanted to leave the woman here alone while he ran to the store, not until he had a better read on the situation.

"If you need anything else, let me know." Ansley took a step back.

"I will. Thanks for being a good little sister."

"What can I say? I am the best." Ansley winked at him.

A smile spread across Jaxon's face. He'd always liked the fire Ansley had inside her. Out of everybody in the family, he and Ansley were the closest. Or, at least, they *had* been.

Jaxon took the bag and stepped back inside. As he did, he caught another glance of Abby. She looked so peaceful as she slept there on the couch, without any signs of the trauma that happened to her earlier.

Whoever she really was and whatever had really happened to her, Jaxon had just opened up his life to a stranger.

Second chance, he reminded himself. This time, he couldn't let himself fail.

CHAPTER EIGHT

I DECIDED to stay in town until I heard the news about Abi-jail. I needed that final burst of pleasure, of satisfaction. In a place the size of Fog Lake, news like someone's death should travel fast.

But I hadn't heard anything, and I didn't like that.

Then again, maybe no one had discovered Abi-jail's body yet. After all, she was out in the middle of nowhere. The animals might get to her before anyone ever did find her.

A smile spread across my face at the thought of it.

But until I had confirmation on her death, I couldn't leave the area. Tomorrow, I would travel to the place I'd last seen her body. I would confirm that she was still there and that she was dead. It was the right thing to do.

And I prided myself in always doing the right thing.

Excitement rolled around inside me, almost like a hamster on a wheel going at full speed. Once news traveled, I should be a hero. But no one would know I'd been the one brave enough to serve justice.

That was okay. I knew.

I grabbed dinner at the local pub in town—a place called Hanky's. It was a dive inside and looked like it hadn't been updated in a couple decades. The inside smelled like grease, and old eighties music played on the overhead.

I took a sip of my iced tea and smiled at a woman sitting at the bar across the restaurant. She was pretty with soft brown hair and a curvy figure. I'd guess her to be in her late thirties. Probably here on business, based on her black skirt and button-up blouse.

I could tell by the way she looked at me that she found me attractive.

I'd been told that before. Some women loved my overbearing confidence, while others found it off-putting. I tried to put the second set of women in their place. Women weren't meant to be empowered. They were meant to be controlled.

I flashed my admirer a smile, acting like I'd left our meeting in her court while secretly knowing that I controlled every part of the situation. It was my area of gifting.

A moment later, she sashayed over and sat across from me. "Anyone sitting here?"

"Now you are." I didn't bother to smile. A smile would make me look weak.

"What brings you this way?" She lowered her head and fluttered her eyelashes, attempting to flirt.

I pushed my half-eaten burger and fries away. It hadn't been that good. If I were a food critic, I would have given this place two rotten tomatoes.

"I had some business to attend to," I told her.

She raised her overly plucked brow. "Business? Oh . . . it sounds like you're important."

I gave her a slight nod. She was smarter than I gave her credit for. "I like to think so."

"I like important men," she cooed.

Suddenly, my evening looked like it might be a little more exciting.

I only hoped she didn't disappoint . . . because then there would be consequences.

CHAPTER NINE

ABBY AWOKE WITH A START. Sweat covered every inch of her skin, and her heart beat so fast she could hardly breathe.

Her gaze skittered across the room. A fire crackled. Log walls stood guard. The rich aroma of coffee floated in the air.

Where . . . ?

That was right. She was at Jaxon Wilder's place.

Abby pushed herself up, a plaid blanket dropping to her waist. She must have fallen asleep on the couch . . . last night.

She raked a hand through her hair. She'd slept hard. Really hard. Harder than she had in weeks, for that matter.

A footfall sounded behind her, and she jumped.

Visions of the Executioner rushed back to her. Of seeing him standing outside her cabin. Of the fear he spread like a poison.

"It's just me."

Jaxon came into focus.

He stood there wearing jeans and a thermal long-sleeved shirt, a cautious look on his face.

Abby sucked in a breath at the sight of him.

She hadn't been delusional last night when she'd thought he was handsome. No, the man was breathtaking in every way. Tall, trim, quiet. He reminded her slightly of a younger Josh Duhamel—and that was a very good thing.

Her cheeks heated when she realized she'd practically passed out on his couch and had stayed there all night. "You should have woken me."

He shrugged nonchalantly. "You were sleeping too soundly."

"I've been . . . tired." Abby offered an apologetic smile, figuring she didn't need to explain anymore.

"I imagine you have." He paused in front of her, hands in his pockets. He looked laid-back and protective at the same time—if that were possible. He somehow managed to pull the dichotomy off. "How are you?"

That was a great question. Abby wasn't sure. Finally, she shrugged. "I don't know."

"Fair enough." He nodded toward the front door. "I was going to drink some coffee on the porch. It's kind of my thing. It helps me clear my head before I start the day. You want to join me?"

"Why not?" She had no reason to refuse. In fact, it sounded kind of refreshing.

"Take the blanket with you, just in case you get cold. I'll grab the coffee."

Abby wrapped the green plaid one around her shoulders like a shawl and stepped outside. She paused, sucking in a breath. Fog Lake stared back at her in all its glory. Just as yesterday, the water was clothed in a thin layer of fog. The low-lying clouds gave the whole area an almost magical feel. She could get used to a view like this.

She sat on one of the wooden steps facing the lake and waited for Jaxon. A moment later, the door opened again, and Jaxon handed her a steaming mug. He lowered himself beside her on the steps.

"How's your head?" Jaxon's question almost sounded casual, like they did this all the time. "Or is it too early to tell?"

"I think it will be fine." Abby raised the steaming mug to her face and let the warmth spread over her skin. "Thank you again for letting me stay here. I don't know how I can repay you, but I will."

"Don't worry about it. I'm not all that concerned myself."

She took a sip of coffee, and the hot liquid washed through her system. Then the taste hit her. This blend wasn't your run-of-the-mill coffee. The flavor was smooth, pleasant, and unique.

"This is good," she said. "Really good."

"Thanks. I actually roasted the beans for this coffee myself. I call it Troops on the Grounds Coffee."

She raised her eyebrows and took another sip. "I love the name. And you should look into doing this on a wider scale."

"I've thought about it."

"I mean it. This is really good. It's nutty and sweet." She got excited just thinking about taking another swallow.

Jaxon smiled. "I'll take that into consideration."

She froze when movement at the edge of the lake caught her eye.

Was that . . . ?

Yes, it was.

Someone was out there. On Jaxon's property. Walking their way.

Abby tried to spot him again, but he disappeared.

Or had she been seeing things?

Abby didn't know. But she couldn't look away.

A second later, a man wearing a black or blue jacket and a ball cap came into view.

The coffee mug slipped from her hands and crashed on the steps. Dark liquid spread everywhere.

"Abby?" Jaxon asked.

She hardly heard him. Was that . . . the Executioner? Would he be this brazen?

Abby knew the answer.

Yes, he would be.

The man moved toward them without urgency—just like the man in the woods yesterday had. That was what made him even scarier—his lack of conscience.

He was coming back to kill her, just like all those threats had foretold.

A deep shiver raked through her body.

"I . . ." She tried to formulate something to say. If that was the Executioner, it wasn't just her in danger right now. Jaxon wasn't safe either.

Abby rose to her feet. In three steps, she had backed up to the door.

Jaxon followed her gaze and saw the man there. At once, things seemed to click in his mind, and he joined Abby. "Do you think that's the man who's been threatening you?"

"I . . . I don't know." She didn't have the answers. She only knew the fear bubbling inside her.

"Why don't you wait in the cabin?"

But Abby could hardly move. All she could do was watch. Her head pounded as she anticipated the pain. The judgment.

Jaxon nudged her into his cabin. "Stay here. Understand?"

She grabbed his arm, realizing he was about to confront this man. He had no idea what he was getting into. "You can't. He's dangerous."

Jaxon stared at her another moment as if trying to get a proper read on the situation. "We don't know that this is our guy."

"But what if it is?" Her voice cracked.

JAXON WASN'T GOING to let someone else bully him or his guest. He grabbed a loaded gun from a drawer in his living room. Making sure Abby was tucked away safe, he opened the front door to step back outside.

"Jaxon . . ." Abby said.

The look in her eyes clutched his heart and transported him back in time. Back to Iraq. Back to—

Not now. He didn't have time to go there. Focus was everything in situations like these.

"I'll be okay," he assured Abby.

"But . . ."

"Stay here."

Bracing himself for a confrontation, Jaxon stepped outside. He closed the door behind him and put his hands on his hips as he watched the man in the distance.

The man certainly didn't move like somebody who was threatening. He seemed to be on a leisurely stroll.

As he got closer, Jaxon noticed that he was probably in his early sixties. He saw the wrinkles on his face, his neat beard, and the salt-and-pepper hair beneath his hat. He reminded Jaxon more of a grandfather . . .

The man offered a smile. "Beautiful day out here, isn't it?"

Jaxon remained on the porch, placing himself

between the door and the man. "It sure is. A little breezy, though."

The man chuckled and took another step closer, still not giving off any type of dangerous vibe. But Jaxon wouldn't let his guard down yet.

"I'm looking for my dog. Name is Hunter, and he's a chocolate lab. You seen him?"

"Sorry, I haven't seen any dogs out here today."

"Well, if you do see him, I'm staying at a cabin about a half a mile from here. He ran away from me when I let him out to go to the bathroom this morning, and he hasn't come back since."

"I'll keep my eyes open," Jaxon said.

The man nodded and tipped his hat. "Thanks, I appreciate it."

Jaxon watched as the man walked away, continuing down the lake. No, he definitely didn't seem threatening. So what was with Abby's reaction?

He waited until the man was out of sight before going back inside. Jaxon's gaze scanned his cabin.

Where had Abby gone? She was nowhere to be seen.

Alarm rushed through him. Had she run? Or had that man looped back around to find her?

CHAPTER TEN

ABBY PRESSED herself against the wall in the closet, muttering prayers. Trying to count backward. Trying to do anything so that fear wouldn't consume her.

What was happening out there? What if that man hurt Jaxon? What if he'd come inside now to finish her?

A moan escaped from her lips. How much longer could she live like this?

If the Executioner had his way, Abby wouldn't have to worry about that much longer.

She pulled her arms closer and waited, listened.

Nothing.

Except . . . were those footprints?

Her heartbeats came faster, harder, louder.

What if it was the killer?

She glanced around, looking for something to defend herself with. There was nothing except some clothes hangers and a vacuum. But maybe . . .

She grabbed one of the attachments on the vacuum.

Just as the door opened, she raised it like a baseball bat and began to swing. A guttural cry escaped from her as she fought back, determined not to let this guy take her too easily.

"Whoa," a deep voice muttered.

The man grabbed her wrists. In one motion, he'd subdued her. Taken away her defenses.

And now she was at his mercy.

Except . . . as the face came into view, she realized it wasn't the Executioner.

"It's just me," Jaxon murmured. "You're okay."

She let out her breath so quickly that she nearly passed out. Only the wall behind her kept her upright. Jaxon took her arm and led her to the couch, his worried gaze on her.

As she settled on the cushions there, Abby's eyes met Jaxon's. "Sorry about that. I suppose I'm on edge."

"It's okay. That man was just looking for his dog. He's gone now."

Abby watched Jaxon's expression, looking for any signs of irritation. She saw only a long, studious gaze. He clearly wanted answers she couldn't give him.

"I suppose I need to call to have my car towed today, so I can get out of your hair."

"You're not in my hair. But I would be happy to call Lewy for you. He's pretty much the only tow truck driver in town."

"I appreciate that." Abby ran a hand through her hair again. "Do you mind if I go clean myself up?"

He handed her a paper sack from the kitchen table. "I had my sister bring a few things over. I figured you would need some clothes and other supplies to get you by. Hopefully there's something in there that you can use."

"Thank you." Abby took the bag from him, thankful for Jaxon's thoughtfulness. "I really appreciate this."

"Just head up the steps and you should be able to figure everything out in the apartment. Or, if you'd prefer, you can use my bathroom downstairs. It has a heated towel holder that's pretty fantastic if I do say so myself."

"I have never been able to resist a heated towel

holder." She flashed a smile. The truth was, the closer she was to Jaxon, the safer she felt.

"Help yourself. There's a hair dryer beneath the sink also and clean towels in the cabinet."

A few minutes later, Abby was under the steady spray of the shower. As she carefully washed her hair, her mind drifted back in time. Drifted to the moment she met Patrick.

It had been a year and a half ago. She was living in Georgia and running her bakery in the quaint downtown area of the Atlanta suburb where she lived. He was in Minnesota. They'd met online and had seemed like a perfect match. After talking on the phone and emailing for four months, they finally decided to meet face-to-face.

From the moment Abby had first laid eyes on Patrick, she'd been smitten. He was a former college football star, with a broad chest and a smile that could melt anyone's heart. He worked in the tech world, and money never seemed to be an issue.

They'd talked nonstop. The two of them seemed to have so much in common that it seemed like the online website where they'd been introduced had some type of magic formula that had proved to be a smashing success.

After that first meeting, their phone calls had

increased. They'd talked nearly every day. A month later, Patrick came to her hometown in Georgia. Abby had shown him around, taken him into her bakery, and introduced him to her friends. Everything seemed so perfect.

Despite the warm spray of the shower, Abby suddenly felt cold.

She and Patrick continued to meet like that over the next six months. Each time they met, her feelings became stronger and stronger until Abby thought that she'd eventually marry this guy.

They had talked about it. They had talked about what they would like their wedding to be like—on the beach. Maybe even Hawaii, with just a few family members and friends. They'd talked about their honeymoon—also in Hawaii. They'd even talked about how many kids they wanted—three was the perfect number, they'd agreed.

After years of being single, after being accused of being too picky, Abby finally felt like she had met her dream guy. Her patience had finally paid off.

She shut the water off and felt the remaining moisture trickle down her skin. As she did, she closed her eyes and lifted her head. What she wouldn't give to go back in time. To know then what she knew today.

But life didn't work like that, and now everything had been turned upside down.

Meeting Patrick had been the worst thing to ever happen to her.

He was the reason she was in this mess right now.

JAXON PUT some bacon on the griddle and, while it sizzled, began cracking some eggs. He had to make breakfast for himself anyway, so why not make enough for both him and Abby? His guest needed to eat.

The incident from earlier today kept replaying in his mind. Abby was obviously shaken after everything that happened, and no one could blame her for that. It had been quite the ordeal she'd gone through. Seeing that stranger outside the cabin had nearly made her have a panic attack.

For a moment, Jaxon considered doing a Google search on her, but he changed his mind. Abby would tell him the truth about what was going on whenever she was ready.

As he began chopping some onions for an omelet, his phone rang. He looked down at the screen and smiled when he saw the number. He hit the speaker button, and his mom's voice came over the line.

"Hello, Son, how are you doing?"

"Doing okay, Mom. How about you?"

"I've been busy with the renovations on the house, but otherwise I'm doing fine. Are we still on for lunch later today?"

With everything going on, it had slipped Jaxon's mind. "Is there any way we could reschedule? Maybe until next week?"

They hadn't missed once in the four months since he'd returned to town. They always chose a location in Pigeon Forge or Gatlinburg, away from the small-town gossips in Fog Lake. It allowed them a small amount of privacy.

"Of course. Is everything okay?"

He set down his knife and flipped the bacon. "Everything is fine. Something just came up that I need to address."

"I'll just check in next week, and we can look at our schedules then, okay?"

"Sounds good, Mom. I love you."

"I love you too."

As he ended the call, his heart pounded.

His brothers and sister didn't know that he was

still in contact with their mom. It was one of the reasons Jaxon felt like he had to leave seven years ago. His mom had betrayed the family so badly that his siblings said they would never forgive her. But, to Jaxon, his mom was his mom. He wanted her in his life, and he knew the power of forgiveness.

Still, he couldn't tell his brothers or sister about it because he knew how they'd feel. Instead, he remained in the middle, pulled between both sides and empathizing with each opposing viewpoint.

He looked up as Abby stepped from the hallway. Her hair was dry and clean, and she wore some of Ansley's old jeans and a flannel shirt. Abby was a very attractive woman. Slender. Petite. Long, silky hair. High cheekbones.

"You look like you're a regular around here," Jaxon said as he poured some eggs onto the skillet and listened as they cooked.

She tugged the red flannel shirt. "The clothes fit perfectly. Thank you." She glanced at the food. "Can I help with anything?"

"Nope. I've got this covered."

She took a seat on the barstool across from him and watched him. "You look like you know what you're doing."

"I always ended up being the designated cook

around my friends. Breakfast became my specialty."
He added some veggies to the omelet.

"It smells great."

He glanced up at her, wondering what she was like beyond the events of yesterday. "How about you? You like to cook?"

"Cook? Not so much. But I love baking."

His honesty meter registered. This wasn't one of her veiled truths, but she was being real with him now. "Is that right? What do you like to bake?"

"Cookies are my specialty. Sugar cookies with icing, for that matter."

"You'll have to make some before you leave if you have time. The previous owner left all kinds of baking supplies—bags and tips and pans. I stuck them up in a cabinet somewhere."

She smiled. "I would love to. Funny enough, I actually went to college on a soccer scholarship."

Another truth. He raised an eyebrow. "Did you?"

"That's right. But I got into the habit of making cookies before our practices and matches. Unfortunately, I spent so much time in the kitchen that I was often late getting to where I needed to be. I ended up losing my scholarship. But I kept all my friends on the team. They kept coming back for the cookies, I suppose." She smiled.

The action looked nice on her.

Jaxon couldn't help but smile also. "If you're going to get kicked off a soccer team, then cookies are good reason for it."

"That's what I always said. My dad didn't quite feel the same way when I lost my scholarship."

"I suppose I can see that also."

He set a plate with bacon and an omelet in front of her. "I'm assuming you eat meat? I really shouldn't assume these types of things these days."

"I do. I love meat. And sugar. And flour. Lots of sugar and flour. I wish I didn't."

"Well, it hasn't seemed to affect your weight so I think you're doing okay."

No, her weight seemed just fine. Not that Jaxon had noticed. But it was hard not to in those jeans and that shirt.

"How long have you been back here in Fog Lake?" Abby picked up her fork.

"About four months."

"Did you decide not to reenlist?"

He swallowed hard, his food not quite as appetizing at the moment. "No, it was just time for me to get out. When you know, you know."

"What have you been doing since you got out?" Abby took a bite of her omelet.

"Sometimes I help out my brother Boone in his store. I do some volunteer firefighting as well. I figure I have some time to sort things out. I have some money saved up, enough that I'll be comfortable for a while."

"It's always good to have time to figure out what you want to do."

They ate for a few minutes in silence. There was so much more that Jaxon wanted to ask, but he didn't want to sound like he was interrogating her again. Why didn't she have anyone in her life to help her? The woman was nice, personable, kind. It didn't make sense.

His phone rang, and he saw Luke's number.

"Excuse me for a minute." Jaxon stepped away and put the phone to his ear. "What's up?"

"Hey, I just got a call from Lewy about Abby's car."

Based on the sound of Luke's voice, something hadn't gone as planned. "Okay ..."

"You're going to want to come down to the station. Bring Abby with you."

CHAPTER ELEVEN

ABBY FELT the anxiety churning in her stomach as she rode with Jaxon to the station. Apparently, the sheriff hadn't given any more details about why he'd summoned them. Either that or Jaxon wasn't sharing. What could have happened that Abby would be needed down at the sheriff's?

Her gut told her it was something bad.

"It's probably nothing to be nervous over." Jaxon seemed to sense her anxiety.

She nodded but said nothing. It was kind of him to try to make her feel better, but nothing could make her feel more relaxed at this point.

A blur of scenic landscape passed the windows. Mountains lined the road, along with barren trees.

Fog still settled in the crevices and near the lake, the clouds sometimes invading the road on this bleak day.

Jaxon pulled his truck in front of the station and put it in Park. As they stepped out, Abby paused on the sidewalk and glanced around.

What if the Executioner was here? What if he was watching her now? A chill swept over her.

Since she had no idea what the man's face looked like, everyone seemed suspect. Plus, this man was smart. He always seemed to know what she was doing, when she was doing it, and what she would do next. It wouldn't surprise her in the least if he had his eyes on her right now.

She shivered again at the thought.

Jaxon appeared beside her and placed his hand on the small of her back. His touch made Abby flinch—not because it was intrusive. It just surprised her.

Either Jaxon didn't notice or he didn't say anything. Instead, he led her inside the sheriff's office. Sheriff Wilder greeted them with a stern glance and nodded that they should follow. Jaxon and Abby walked through the station to a back lot.

Every step made Abby's stomach tighten even

more. The beat-up sedan she'd borrowed from an old friend waited outside. Nothing looked amiss about it, at least from this angle. Abby could see that the tires were still flat, but the back window was intact and not shattered.

So why had Sheriff Wilder called her out here?

"When Lewy got there to tow your car this morning, a message had been left on the windshield," Sheriff Wilder started.

Abby felt the blood drain from her face. "Is that right?"

"Unfortunately, yes."

She and Jaxon followed the sheriff to the front of the vehicle. What she saw there made her head spin.

The word KILLER had been written in what appeared to be blood. Remnants of each letter dripped down the windshield, sending terror through anyone looking at it.

Abby got the message loud and clear. The Executioner was still here in town. He knew she was alive, and he was still looking for her, determined to spread his own brand of justice into her life.

"Any idea why someone would do this?" Sheriff Wilder turned to Abby, studying her face unapologetically.

Her mind raced. Maybe she should tell them. Tell them everything.

But she knew how things would change if she did that. People here wouldn't look at her the same way, and she couldn't blame them.

That was why she decided to stay silent on the matter.

"It must be the man who's been coming after me." She rubbed her throat, feeling the burn inside. "He goes by the Executioner."

Disappointment—and skepticism—flooded the sheriff's gaze. "You failed to mention anything about this earlier."

"I know . . . and I'm sorry."

He stared at her another moment before saying, "I'm going to need some more information on him."

"Of course," Abby said. "Anything you need."

Even as she said the words, she knew that it wasn't *anything* that he needed. Abby was going to have to choose her words wisely.

And it was a shame. She'd enjoyed getting to know Jaxon this morning. But her time in Fog Lake would be coming to an end.

She needed to figure out a way to get out of town. How she was going to do that, she didn't know. But there had to be a way.

~

JAXON SAT beside Abby in Luke's office. The message left on her windshield had been unnerving, to say the least. Had it been written in blood?

He had no idea. The liquid would need to be tested. And, even if the substance was blood, it wasn't necessarily human.

But that didn't make Jaxon feel any better.

"When did you first start receiving these threats from the man referred to as the Executioner?" Luke sat at his desk, an intimidating figure. It came with the job, though part of Jaxon wished he'd cut Abby some slack. She'd already been through a lot.

Abby rubbed her hands against her jeans. Jaxon thought some color had begun coming back to her cheeks earlier this morning. But now she looked paler than ever. Seeing that message would have shaken anyone.

"It started about two months ago. This man goes by the name of Judge, Jury, and Executioner. I guess I just shortened it to the Executioner."

Disgust trickled through Jaxon. Whoever this person was they were dealing with, he was sick. Totally sick.

"Tell us about the first time you ever heard from him," Luke said.

Abby drew in a long, shaky breath. "The first time I heard from him was through an email. He said he knew who I was and that he would personally see to it that I paid for my sins."

"Any idea what that means?" Luke tilted his head.

Jaxon knew his brother. He was not only listening to every word Abby said, but he was also watching her body language, looking for any sign she wasn't telling the truth. Their dad had taught them how to be observant. He'd been sheriff here before Luke—before cancer had taken him away too early.

"I've made my fair share of mistakes in life, but he never said anything specific about how I was a sinner," Abby said.

Was Abby being vague on purpose? Jaxon wondered. That's what Jaxon had to assume.

"What happened next?" Luke asked.

"I kept getting the same type of emails, with the same types of threats."

"Did you go to the police?"

Abby shrugged. "They didn't seem all that concerned, especially since nothing else happened."

"Then what?" Luke continued.

"I began getting text messages also. Somehow, this man got my phone number. Somebody began following me. I thought I was just being paranoid, especially since I never saw anyone's face and nothing specific happened. But the feeling always remained with me." She ran a trembling hand through her hair.

Luke picked up a pen and jotted something on a pad of paper in front of him. "Do you still have copies of these messages or texts?"

Abby swallowed so hard that Jaxon saw her throat tighten. "I deleted them."

"And why would you do that?"

Abby shrugged and began rubbing her hands on her jeans again. She seemed to do that when she was nervous. "They bothered me. I found myself staring at them all the time. And, like I said, the police in my hometown didn't seem to be willing to help me."

Why would the police ignore those threats? Jaxon wondered. It didn't make sense.

"Is your computer with you?" Luke asked. "Maybe we can still access them."

"I left my computer and my phone back at home."

Jaxon glanced at his brother's face and saw the

doubt in his eyes. This wasn't going the way Luke had hoped. Jaxon, too, had hoped Abby might be forthcoming with her answers, but that didn't appear to be the case. Despite that, the picture that formed wasn't a good one.

"Did things continue to escalate?" Luke asked.

"I came home from work one day and noticed that someone had been in my apartment. I didn't think anything was taken, but later I found a snake hiding under my bed." She shivered as she talked about it. "I had to call an exterminator to get rid of it. It was poisonous."

Instead of rubbing her jeans, she touched her head. Jaxon remembered the doctor's instructions. She was supposed to take it easy.

This didn't qualify.

"Anything else?" Luke's eagle-eyed gaze remained on her.

Abby drew a deep breath. "I kept having the feeling that somebody was coming and going from my place. I even had the locks changed. After a while, I went to stay with a friend. I continued to get emails and texts and to feel like somebody was watching me. Also, the threats became more detailed. This man talked about what he was going to do when he finally decided to exact his judgment on me."

Luke leaned forward "And what was that?"

"He was going to break one of my bones for every sin I'd ever committed. He was going to keep me alive so he could delight in my cries of pain. And he would make an example of me for all the world to see."

CHAPTER TWELVE

JAXON AND LUKE met in the hallway after Luke finished questioning Abby.

"So what do you think?" Luke asked, his gaze on Jaxon.

There was a time when Luke would have never asked for Jaxon's opinion. Maybe things had changed while he'd been away. Maybe he was no longer viewed as just a little brother.

"There's obviously something she's still hiding," Jaxon finally said.

Luke rubbed his jaw. "That's what I think too. But what? Everything she said was so horrific. I can't imagine what she wouldn't be telling us."

"Maybe there's some kind of sin she's ashamed to mention."

"Possibly."

"Either way, the danger this woman is in is real."

Luke glanced down at his phone and frowned again.

"Everything okay?" Jaxon asked. Whatever message was there had obviously distracted Luke from his investigation into Abby. What else could possibly be going on?

"A woman here in town with a corporate getaway for her law firm disappeared last night. None of her colleagues have seen her since then, and they're getting worried."

"Doesn't she have to be gone for twenty-four hours before you can do anything?"

"That's what people say, but we will initiate something sooner if we feel the need. That's what we're going to have to do here. Her car is still at her chalet, and she's not answering her cell phone. Everyone says this isn't like her."

"It sounds like you have a full plate today."

"Yes, not to mention that we have Harper's birthday party tomorrow night. You're still coming, right?"

"Of course. I wouldn't miss it for the world." Jaxon shifted. "So what are you going to do about Abby?"

Luke frowned and glanced at his office, where Abby waited. "All I know to do is to continue investigating and keep my eyes open. I sent one of my guys over to her cabin to see if there was any other evidence there. I hope to hear back from him soon."

"Is she free to go?"

"She's free to go. Are you going to let her keep staying at your place?" Luke studied Jaxon's gaze, and he almost felt like he was being tested.

Jaxon shrugged. "I don't mind if she uses the apartment above mine. It seems a shame to let it sit empty when she needs help."

Luke nodded, as if he wasn't surprised. "Just be careful."

"You think she's dangerous?" Jaxon honestly wanted to know what Luke was thinking. His brother was more objective in this situation than he was.

"I didn't say that. But, like we both said, she's hiding something. We don't know what that information is."

Jaxon nodded, unable to argue with his brother's assessment. "Will do. I'll keep an eye on her. Especially until we know what's going on."

He hoped he didn't regret it.

ABBY JERKED her head up as Jaxon and Luke stepped back into the office. She could only imagine the conversation they'd been having. No doubt, it had centered around what she'd just told them.

Did they buy her story? She'd told them the truth—just not all of it.

Guilt pressed in on her at the thought, but she needed to stand by her convictions. As a matter of self-preservation, there were some details she needed to keep quiet.

She wasn't good at playing games. Her natural inclination was to be an open book and freely share details about her life.

That would be foolish right now, though.

"Listen, how about we grab a bite to eat?" Jaxon suggested. "We didn't finish our breakfast, and it's lunchtime now."

"I don't have my purse . . ."

"I can cover you."

That wasn't even her biggest concern. Being out in public brought an entirely different kind of anxiety. However, with Jaxon by her side, she somehow felt safer. Which was ridiculous. She didn't know the man. She shouldn't depend on him. Yet, part of her already trusted him.

She and Jaxon walked down the street. The day around them was still gray, and something in the air seemed to promise snow soon. She tightened the scarf that Jaxon had loaned her, thankful for the warmth.

Two blocks later they reached the Hometown Diner. The inside looked like she had stepped back in time to the sixties, and it smelled like all the goodness of her childhood. French fries and hamburgers and sizzling crispy chicken tenders.

"It's not much, but it's one of my favorite places to grab a bite of comfort food here in town." Jaxon followed her gaze. "I figured some comfort food might do the job right now."

"Sounds great," Abby said.

They were seated at a booth in the corner of the room as strands of The Contours' "Do You Love Me?" played from the jukebox.

A few minutes later, Abby had ordered a crispy chicken sandwich with buffalo sauce and some french fries with ranch. The meal wouldn't be great for her waistline, but her mouth was watering for it. Comfort food sounded like the perfect remedy right now.

Abby hadn't eaten much over the past week. Suddenly her appetite was coming back strong. Which made no sense. She'd think she wouldn't want to eat anything after seeing that cryptic message left on her car.

She shoved the thought aside and tried to pretend this was just a normal lunch with a new friend. A moment of normal might do her a world of good.

"Is this your first time in Fog Lake?" Jaxon asked before taking a sip of his sweet tea.

"It is. I've been to Gatlinburg before but never Fog Lake. But I've always heard good things about it."

"It's quite the place. In the summer, people camp, fish, zipline, and hike. The lake is busy with watersports and houseboats. Then there's the fall . . . when the leaves are changing and the harvest festival takes place, Fog Lake is *the* place to be."

"I just saw the advertisement for a Hills, Hollows, and Hearts celebration . . ." Abby had passed some signs on the street corner advertising the Valentine's Day event as they'd walked here.

"That's something new that the town is trying this year," Jaxon said. "They are going to set up some outside heaters and some bonfires. A local band,

Rosie and the Men Who Stole My Land, is going to open for Dirk Watson."

"The country singer?"

"He's buying a cabin out in this area and offered to do the concert for free."

"Nice."

"It should be. There will be food and a dance in the town square. It should be a good time."

"It sounds charming." It was too bad that Abby wouldn't be here for that. Or, even if she was, no way she would find herself enjoying an evening like that —not with the imminent threats she faced.

She hadn't enjoyed herself in such a long time. For that matter, she couldn't even remember when the last time was. If Abby had to guess, it would be the last date she and Patrick had together. They'd met down in the Florida Keys—Patrick had paid— and they'd gone snorkeling.

That seemed like another lifetime . . . or a bad dream.

"With this town's history, it's good to find some joy, you know?" Jaxon continued.

Abby realized he was still talking about the Valentine's celebration. "The town's history?" she questioned.

Jaxon shrugged. "You heard about the Native American massacre here, right?"

"Now that you mention it, it does sound vaguely familiar."

"It was terrible. A lot of people feel like this town will never be the same because of it."

A pretty woman with curly dark hair wandered over to them just then. She was dressed like a businesswoman in her black slacks and button-up blouse. Her eyes were warm on Jaxon's.

Abby wondered if this might be someone Jaxon was interested in. Certainly someone like Jaxon had a long line of women waiting to date him. She'd yet to see one reason he'd still be single.

"Hey, Jax." The woman paused at their booth. "Good to see you out and about." The woman's gaze turned to Abby, and she extended her hand along with a wide smile. "I'm Harper, Jaxon's sister-in-law."

"And Sheriff Wilder's wife," Jaxon added.

Abby sat up a little straighter. "It's nice to meet you. I'm Abby."

"Nice to meet you. I was just grabbing lunch to go." She held up the bag in her hands. "I saw you over here and wanted to swing by to say hello. By the way, I heard about that missing woman."

Missing woman? What was she talking about?

"Scary, huh?" Jaxon glanced at Abby, as if trying to read her expression.

"I hope they find her. The attorney who organized the retreat has called Luke multiple times as well as City Hall. He's not going to let this drop until she'd found." Harper shook her head. "Anyway, I'll talk to you two later. Nice to meet you, Abby."

After Harper left, Abby looked back at Jaxon. "Missing woman?"

"It could be nothing."

"It doesn't sound like nothing."

Jaxon shrugged. "Luke is handling it."

Abby forced herself to nod and drop the subject. Jaxon obviously didn't want to talk about it. But curiosity burned in her mind. Could this be connected?

"Harper seems nice," Abby finally said.

"She's very nice. Luke was really lucky to find her. She's a former journalist, but now she helps out with public relations here in town. I am nearly certain Hills, Hollows, and Hearts was her brainchild."

Journalist? Abby hoped the woman didn't still have a nose for story leads. If so, Abby had walked right into the middle of trouble.

She hardly had time to think about it, though.

Across the restaurant, Abby felt someone's gaze on her and tensed. She scanned the patrons inside, searching for the source of her discomfort.

Her eyes stopped on a man sitting by himself in the diner.

She hadn't been imagining things. The man, probably in his late forties, sat on the other side of the room. When he saw Abby looking, he quickly glanced away.

He fit a basic description of the Executioner. He was the same height and stature. Probably the same age, and definitely the same ethnicity. He didn't have a beard, but he could have shaved.

Abby tried to pull herself together before her actions revealed too much of her and her thoughts. She didn't want Jaxon asking more questions. However, if this man was the Executioner, not only was she in danger right now, but so was Jaxon.

Suddenly, her appetite disappeared.

Just as the thought entered her mind, the waitress set their food in front of them. Jaxon lifted up a prayer before digging into his burger. Abby picked at her fries, but her gaze continually went back to the man across the restaurant. Whenever he thought Abby wasn't watching, he stared at her again.

"Is that man giving you trouble?" Jaxon asked.

Abby should have known that he was studying her, watching her expressions and practically reading her thoughts. The man was too observant for his own good.

"It's nothing," she insisted. "I'm just on edge."

"Do you recognize that man?" Jaxon obviously wasn't buying her excuse.

"I don't. But I did notice him watching me. Doesn't mean anything."

Jaxon's hard gaze crossed the room. Abby looked back at the man again and saw him turn back to the newspaper in his hands.

Unease sloshed inside her.

In a situation like this, how exactly did she know whom to trust?

CHAPTER THIRTEEN

JAXON NEEDED TO MAKE A CHOICE. Should he confront the stranger across the restaurant, or wait to see how things played out?

He'd been watching the man also, and he'd seen him looking at Abby. The man looked harmless on the outside, like a businessman having a casual lunch. Nothing about him screamed menacing. But that didn't mean he *was* innocent. Nor did it mean he was guilty.

Just as Jaxon started to rise from the booth to strike up a conversation with the man, his phone buzzed. He looked down and saw a text from Ansley.

SHE'S THE OTHER WOMAN.

. . .

WHAT IN THE world was his sister talking about? He typed back:

???

BEFORE HE COULD SEE Ansley's reply, the man across the restaurant stood and strode toward them. Jaxon bristled, waiting for trouble and preparing himself to act.

Across from him, Abby froze. Her breathing became fast, shallow. Sweat sprinkled across her forehead.

The man offered a sympathetic smile as he approached. "I'm sorry to be staring. It's just that you look like someone familiar."

Abby offered a weak smile, but her breathing seemed to even out some. "I get that a lot."

"I could tell I was making you uncomfortable, so I wanted to apologize. I was just trying to place who I thought you might be."

"Don't worry about it," Abby rushed.

The man's gaze lingered on her a moment longer

before he nodded and took a step back. "Well, enjoy your lunches. I'm sorry to interrupt."

As he walked away, Jaxon turned to Abby. "At least you can rest easy knowing that now, right?"

Abby nodded, but the action seemed too quick. "That's right."

She dipped the french fry into some ranch dressing and put it in her mouth, though she didn't seem that interested in eating it. A surge of compassion rose in Jaxon. The woman was on edge. He knew from experience it was a terrible way to live.

Jaxon looked down at his phone again and saw that Ansley had texted again

PATRICK FINNEGAN.

HE TEXTED BACK:

WHO IS PATRICK FINNEGAN?

HE'D NEVER HEARD the name before, though Ansley obviously assumed he had. As he waited for

Ansley's response he glanced up at Abby. Her gaze fluttered around the restaurant as if she expected trouble to appear any minute.

"Sorry. My sister is texting me. She likes to do that. A lot."

A weak smile played on her lips. "I guess you're not much of a texter?"

"Small talk has never really been my thing whether it's spoken or written, I suppose."

"I was always told I had a gift for chitchat. I haven't felt very chatty lately, though."

Jaxon's phone buzzed again.

HAVE **you been hiding under a rock?**

JAXON CHUCKLED BEFORE TYPING:

DOES IRAQ COUNT AS A ROCK?

ANSLEY IMMEDIATELY RESPONDED.

.   .   .

POINT TAKEN. **I'll tell you more in a second. My 12:00 meeting just got here.**

GREAT. Jaxon was going to have to remain in suspense as to who this Patrick Finnegan and the other woman was. Knowing Ansley, it was the latest celebrity gossip or something. She had a tendency to text him random things throughout the day. She said it was her love language.

They finished the rest of their meal, and Jaxon put some cash on the table.

"I'll repay you." Abby frowned, as if she felt genuinely guilty about having no money. "My purse is back at the house."

"I'm not really worried about it. It's only seven or eight bucks."

"I know, but I don't like to take advantage of people. As soon as I get my wallet, I'll make this right."

Even though Jaxon didn't care about being paid back, he said nothing. If it made Abby feel better to give him some cash for the meal, then so be it.

As his phone rang, he glanced down, halfway expecting it to be Ansley, calling him this time to school him on who Patrick Finnegan was. Instead it was Luke.

"Can you come back down to the station?" Luke asked. "Are you close?"

"Sure, we're just down the street at the Hometown Diner. What's going on?"

"I'd rather tell you in person. Bring Abby with you. I have more questions for her."

Based on Luke's tone, it was more bad news.

ABBY FELT another rush of nerves flutter through her as Jaxon ushered her back to the sheriff's office. What had the sheriff discovered now? Part of her didn't even want to know. This nightmare seemed never-ending.

This was her mess, and she couldn't expect anybody else to figure it out for her. But the possibility of her getting out of town easily was becoming harder by the moment.

She supposed she might be able to call her best friend, Renee, or her father to pick her up. But the last thing Abby wanted to do was to pull them into the middle of this situation. Besides, her father was so disappointed in her. She'd expected, of all people, that he would be on her side. But, instead, he'd looked at her with accusation in his eyes.

The memory of that still caused a rush of grief to crush Abby's heart. One never knew how a person would react in a situation like this until it happened to them. Some of the people she'd thought would stand by her had done the exact opposite. The realization was still hard to stomach.

When they got back to the sheriff's office, Sheriff Wilder looked equally as grim as he had earlier. A doomsday premonition nagged at her—if she believed in premonitions.

"I'd like to talk to you in my office, Ms. Michaels." He gave Jaxon a pointed look. "Alone."

Jaxon nodded and took a seat in one of the chairs in the lobby. "I'll just wait out here then, if that's okay."

With a wave of his hand, Sheriff Wilder ushered Abby into his office.

With every second that passed, her nerves tightened. He'd discovered something about her, hadn't he?

The sheriff sat down behind his desk and directed her into the chair across from him. "I am not going to mince words. I sent a deputy over to your cabin to see if there was any evidence there from when someone left that message on your car. When he went into the cabin where you were staying, he found blood. A lot of blood."

The air left her lungs. "What do you mean, blood?"

The sheriff's gaze narrowed. "I mean, your cabin is now a crime scene."

Her head pounded as his words echoed in her mind. Her cabin? A crime scene? How was that possible? What had happened there?

She swung her head back and forth, trying to make sense of things. The task felt impossible. "When I arrived yesterday, everything looked normal—except the front door was open. Ask Jaxon. He was there when I went back after the hospital."

He shifted, his intimidating gaze never leaving Abby. "Don't worry. I plan on talking to him. So what you're telling me is that you have no idea how that blood got there?"

Abby squeezed the skin between her eyes, wishing she could wake up and discover none of this had been real. "I have no idea. I haven't been back there. I've been with your brother this whole time."

The sheriff stared at her, his gaze unwavering and daring her to make up another lie. "What is it that you're not telling us?"

What should she do? Somebody could have been hurt or murdered at her place. How could she remain silent when that truth was out there? Abby knew the answer.

She couldn't. As strong as her self-preservation was, she had to look at the bigger picture. Doing so might cost her everything. But she couldn't live with herself if she didn't.

She sucked in a deep breath and began telling the sheriff the whole story. With every new fact she revealed, a little part of her died inside.

CHAPTER FOURTEEN

JAXON PULLED out his phone as he waited for Luke to question Abby. What in the world was all this about? He couldn't even begin to imagine. But he knew that Luke had sent a deputy over to Abby's cabin. Had they discovered something?

The reality of the situation pressed on him harder until he felt like he could hardly breathe.

Nailah slammed into his mind.

She'd asked Jaxon for help. Pleaded with him.

As she'd raised her hands to cover her ears as a helicopter passed over, her sleeves fell down. He'd seen the bruises there.

The fact that Jaxon had seen more than the skin exposed around her hijab would have been reason enough for more punishment. If Nailah's husband caught her talking to Jaxon . . . she'd be as good as dead. She'd taken a huge risk by finding him.

"Take me with you," she'd whispered.

"I can't do that." Jaxon didn't even know the woman. Not really. He was stationed in this town to guard this compound where a known terrorist leader lived. Or a former terrorist leader, he should say.

Jaxon had his doubts.

Supposedly, the man was supplying the US with intel.

All Jaxon could see was crookedness. But his job required following orders, not asking questions.

Jaxon released a heavy sigh and pulled up the search bar on his phone's browser. He started to type in "Patrick Finnegan" but stopped himself.

If Abby wanted to tell him then she would.

When Ansley had asked him if he had been hiding under a rock, he knew that was partly the truth. Since he had come back from Iraq, he'd had little desire to watch the news or read the newspaper.

He knew the grim reality of the world around him, and it wasn't something he wanted to remind himself of more than needed. He'd seen the evil that was out there. He'd seen the problems that existed between countries and powers that be. At times, he felt helpless. And he hated feeling helpless.

Just like he had with Nailah . . .

Finally, nearly an hour later, the door to Luke's office opened and Abby stepped out. Her eyes were red, as if she'd been crying.

Something rose inside Jaxon. He wanted to reach out to her, to see if she was okay. Even though they hardly knew each other, he felt some kind of unusual bond with the woman. Perhaps it was everything she'd gone through, and everything that he'd gone through with her, that made him feel this way. Either way, Jaxon knew that this woman needed somebody. No one should have to walk through this kind of trauma alone.

"The sheriff would like to see you." Abby's voice trembled as she spoke. Whatever the conversation had been in there, it had shaken her up. More tension turned in his gut.

Head down low, she started down the hallway toward the bathroom. Before she slipped past, Jaxon gently grasped her arm.

She flinched, as if shocked by his touch.

Jaxon pulled his hand back. "Are you okay?"

She stared at him a minute, almost as if she wanted to say more but couldn't. Finally, she shook her head. "No, I'm not okay. But thank you for asking."

With that last cryptic thought in mind, Jaxon slipped into Luke's office and closed the door. He couldn't deny the tautness of his muscles as he lowered himself into the seat across from his brother.

"What's going on? Abby looks beside herself out there."

"As she should. She's been through a lot."

What did that mean?

Before Jaxon could ask, Luke continued. "I have a few questions for you."

"Ask away." Jaxon had never shied away from the truth. Unless it involved his mother, he supposed. Guilt bit at him for a moment, but he pushed the emotion aside. In that case, he was only trying to avoid unnecessary drama.

"Tell me about what happened when you went back to Abby's cabin yesterday to pick up her car." Luke's voice sounded hard and all business.

Jaxon shifted in his seat and flashed back in time to that moment. "We got there, and Abby started to walk inside. I stopped her and suggested she let me check it out first. She didn't argue. The front door was cracked open just barely."

"And when you got inside?"

He remembered the simple cabin. A paperback novel and cold cup of coffee on the table. "Nothing looked out of place. I figured maybe Abby forgot to latch the door when she went out for her walk." As Jaxon said the word, a sour taste formed in his throat. He knew she didn't just go out for a walk. He wasn't naïve. But, for the sake of simplicity, he left it at that.

"Then what happened?"

"Then I saw her car tires had been slashed. That's when I knew that she was going to need some help. I took her back to my place until she could figure things out."

"Since then has she been out of your sight?"

"Not for more than five minutes I'd say." Jaxon shifted in the seat. "Why? What are you getting at here?"

Luke's jaw tightened. "I can't tell you."

"What do you mean you can't tell me?" Why was his brother being so cryptic?

"What I mean is that some of this information is pertaining to an ongoing investigation. I can't share those details."

Jaxon pushed himself up in his seat as his

thoughts raced. "Did you find something at Abby's place?"

Luke frowned, and Jaxon knew he had hit the nail on the head.

"What did you find?" Jaxon pressed. Certainly his brother knew he could trust him.

Luke glanced to the left and right, even though there was no one else in the room. Finally, he leaned closer. "Between you and me, there was blood in her house. A lot of blood."

"Blood? What do you mean blood?" Jaxon tried to imagine it, but he pushed away the picture that tried to form.

"I mean, it looks like somebody was attacked in her place. And when I say attacked, I mean murdered. There's no way anybody could've lost that amount of blood and survived."

Jaxon's heart pounded in his ears. "Could it have been an animal?"

"The medical examiner is there now, as well as the Tennessee Bureau of Investigation. They'll investigate the blood spatter but, based on what I know, the patterns that were left do not fit an animal attack."

"So, what you're saying is that sometime between yesterday when we went to the cabin and this morning when you sent your deputy out, something horrible happened there?"

"Yes, that's exactly what I'm saying."

Jaxon leaned back and shook his head. "What do you think about these threats Abby's been receiving? What if this guy came back and did this while she was gone? Maybe he was angry because she survived, because she escaped?"

"That's a possibility." Luke stayed silent.

Jaxon shifted again, reading between the lines. "There's more that you are not telling me, isn't there?"

"There's more to her story, just as I suspected."

"What else is there?"

"That's all I can tell you, Jaxon. I've already told you too much. Any more Abby's going to have to tell you herself."

Jaxon chomped down, not liking that answer. "Is she free to go?"

"She is not a suspect, thanks to your alibi. But she is someone we're keeping an eye on, at least until I learn more details of the story."

Jaxon's gut continued to twist. What could Abby possibly have done that would make his brother react like this? Jaxon couldn't even begin to fathom what that might be.

He stood. "Just one more question. Did you find a dead body? Do you know whose blood that was?"

Luke's frown deepened. "No, but we have guys out there looking right now to see what else we can find."

Jaxon didn't like the sound of that. There could've been another murder here in Fog Lake. What was it about this town that seemed to attract danger and anguish?

Jaxon didn't know. He didn't believe in generational curses. But with this town's morbid history, sometimes he did have to wonder . . .

"I'll get Abby and go then."

Luke's pointed gaze met his. "She has orders to stay in town."

"She has to stay in town?" Then she was definitely a person of interest in *something*. But what those details were, Jaxon couldn't imagine.

"And Jaxon?" Luke gave him another look, this one clearly as his big brother. "Be careful."

ABBY EMPTIED the contents of her stomach into the toilet. She'd told the sheriff everything, and he'd intently listened to every word. She'd watched his expression change from curious to disgusted. Doubt had been planted in his mind, just as she thought it would.

Even though the sheriff had remained professional, Abby had felt the wall go up. Not that they had been friendly before, but something had definitely changed. Now he was in there talking to Jaxon.

Her stomach roiled at the thought. Jaxon had been so kind to her. Now he was going to think she was the devil.

She pressed a paper towel over her mouth, her face.

Maybe she should have told him sooner. She supposed she'd been delaying the inevitable and taking a brief reprieve from the nightmare of the last few months.

She rinsed her mouth out and splashed some water on her face.

When she looked in the mirror, Abby hardly recognized the person there. The toll stress could put on a person was no joke. Her skin no longer looked bright and youthful. Her hair looked dull. Her lips even seemed thinner.

But it was her eyes that she noticed the most. At one time, they'd sparkled with life. Now, they just looked hopeless.

Hopeless . . . it was a word Abby had tried not to hang onto. But as more and more time passed, the word only seemed appropriate. The situation she was in had bombarded her from so many different directions. She wasn't sure how she would ever recover.

Then she thought about Theresa, and guilt flooded her. How could Abby even complain about her current circumstances after knowing what had happened to that woman? Abby's circumstances might be bad, but at least she had a chance to make things right. Theresa had been silenced . . . forever.

Abby shoved the thoughts aside and forced herself from the bathroom. When she stepped into the lobby, she saw Jaxon wasn't out there. He must still be meeting with his brother.

What was his brother telling him? Abby had no idea. Because of confidentiality, she didn't think Sheriff Wilder would tell Jaxon all the details she'd shared. But Abby couldn't be sure. Either way, she was going to have to confront this truth sooner rather than later.

Before she could even sit down, Jaxon stepped out. She held her breath as he glanced at her.

Nothing really changed in his gaze, except maybe he looked more curious than he had before.

The sheriff obviously had not told him everything about her history. She released the air from her lungs.

She was going to have to do that herself. It was the way it should be. She hoped she could wait until they had a moment of privacy before she shared all the details, that he didn't demand them sooner.

Jaxon stepped toward her. "Maybe we should go back to my cabin."

She nodded, disliking the numbness that tried to spread over her. "That sounds good."

They said nothing as they stepped out onto the sidewalk. Jaxon walked her to his truck and made sure she was seated inside. But, before he shut the door, his gaze stopped at something in the distance.

"Stay right here and lock the doors." His voice turned hard.

Abby sucked in a deep breath. What was going on? Had Jaxon seen the Executioner? It didn't seem like her tormentor to show his face in public but . . . what did she know?

She didn't ask any questions. As Jaxon slammed the door, she quickly hit the lock and then waited and prayed as he took off down the street.

CHAPTER FIFTEEN

JAXON SAW the shadow figure again. Was this the man who had been threatening Abby? Had he come to the hospital to find her and then followed her here? The timeline fit.

Knowing what he did now about the blood at Abby's cabin, he didn't want to take any chances. Before the man could get away again, Jaxon tore down the street after him. But the man had a head start again. Jaxon had been nearly a block away.

He would do everything in his power to catch the man this time.

Jaxon's muscles burned as he pushed himself faster and faster on the sidewalk. People moved out of his way, casting curious glances as Jaxon quickly maneuvered through the crowds.

He stopped near a corner. The man had disappeared. Again.

But he couldn't have gone far. The question was, where had the man gone exactly?

As Jaxon glanced down one of the side streets, he spotted him again.

Without wasting any time, Jaxon took off that way, barely missing an oncoming car as he raced across the street. Whoever this man was, he was hiding something. Why else would he be running?

The man was nimble. Jaxon had always been a fast runner, and he was having trouble catching the guy now.

As the man turned the corner around another building, Jaxon slowed his steps. He didn't want to walk into a trap. Instead, he braced himself.

As Jaxon rounded the corner, he planted his feet, ready to be jumped.

No one was there.

His gaze wandered down the perimeter of the space. A car in the distance roared to life.

The vehicle was too far away for Jaxon to get the license number, but he noted that it was a black Volvo.

At least this chase hadn't been a total waste.

He drew in several deep breaths, trying to gather his thoughts.

He needed to get back to Abby. He'd left one tumultuous situation only to return to another. As he walked back toward his truck, his phone rang, and Ansley's name popped onto his screen.

He briefly considered not answering, but finally he put the device to his ear. "Hey, Sis. What's up?"

"Hey, Bro. I just got out of my meeting. I wanted to finish the conversation I started earlier."

Jaxon almost told Ansley not to tell him whatever it was she'd discovered. Part of him didn't even want to know what was going on with Abby. Something in his gut told him that this new information would change things. Maybe he didn't want things to change.

Before he could say anything else, Ansley blurted, "Abby is the woman whose boyfriend killed his wife so they could be together."

Jaxon felt the air leave his lungs. "What?"

"Yes, it's been all over the news. If you would watch it, you would know. That's why she looked familiar to me."

Maybe that's why Abby had looked familiar to the man in the restaurant as well. But there was no way Jaxon could see Abby being involved with something like that.

"You have to have it wrong. Abby would never do something like that."

"I'm just telling you what the news is reporting. I don't know who this chick is, and I don't know what she's up to, but be careful."

"I am always careful," Jaxon said.

"But, if the media is right, this woman is like a black widow. She has mind-control power over men. I have a bad feeling about this."

His jaw flexed as he bit down. "You haven't even met her."

"After what I read, I don't need to."

Jaxon put his phone away, but the bad feeling continued to churn in his gut. Obviously, there was a lot more to Abby's story. Jaxon couldn't have been that bad a judge of character, could he?

He didn't know. He didn't want to think so. But Abby was going to need to tell him the truth. He wanted to hear her side of the story. He hoped with everything within him that she had a good explanation as to what had really happened.

As Jaxon spotted his truck in the distance, he saw a car headed toward it. A black Volvo.

He sucked in a breath, expecting the worst.

But the car kept on going.

Strange. Had the driver not known Abby was inside? Or was this mystery person not coming around because of Abby at all?

As soon as Jaxon climbed into his truck, he felt the tension there. It was like Abby knew that he knew the truth.

"Is everything okay?" Abby's voice sounded so sweet, so sincere. Someone like Abby couldn't possibly be guilty of the things she had been accused of.

"I thought I saw someone," Jaxon said. "I thought I saw him at the hospital also."

"Did you catch him?" Abby stared at him with wide eyes.

"No, he got away again."

"Do you think he's the same man who's been sending me threats?"

Jaxon shook his head. "I have no idea who he is, but I do know that he didn't show up until you were in the hospital."

More color left her face, as if that was even possible.

As he started his truck, he turned to Abby. "You and I need to talk."

With a frown, Abby nodded. "You're right. We do.

There are things I should've told you earlier. I'm ready to tell you now."

ABBY WAITED until she was back at Jaxon's cabin with a cup of coffee in her hand and the fire blazing in front of them before sharing her story. She prayed she could get through this without throwing up again, but she wasn't certain that was possible. The emotional impact of everything that had happened felt ingrained into the fiber of her being.

Jaxon sat silently in the chair beside the couch, waiting for her to start. But she could see the hesitation in his gaze and knew this probably wouldn't go well. If she were in Jaxon's shoes, she would also be very hesitant right now. In fact, she would probably run.

She drew in a deep breath and set her cup down, knowing she would be unable to drink yet. There was no good way to start. She just needed to dive in.

"About a year ago my friends encouraged me to try online dating," she said. "They're all married and happy right now, and I'm currently the only single one of the group. So they signed me up, and I really didn't think much of it. I had some guys try to contact me, but I wasn't interested in any of them. Then one day I got a new message from somebody out of state. From the very first line, I was hooked."

"What was his first line?"

"Don't you hate online dating? I did—until I read your profile." Repeating it now, the message seemed a little cheesy. But it had been a refreshing change from the other emails where the guys had tried too hard to sell themselves or they'd been entirely inappropriate.

Jaxon nodded, letting her know he was listening.

"We had a lot in common," Abby continued. "We started emailing, and then it turned into texting, which then turned into talking on the phone. Finally, after a few months, we decided to meet somewhere neutral. We went out to San Antonio, got two separate rooms at a hotel there, and that night we met for the first time for dinner."

She glanced up at Jaxon and saw his face was stoic. He was listening to her every word, but she couldn't get a read on his expression. She had no choice but to continue.

"The first meeting went so well that we decided to meet again the next month. Every time we met those first several times, it was somewhere neutral, and we both got our own rooms. We really clicked, and it was unlike anything I have ever experienced before. He was a businessman. Divorced—his wife had cheated, he said. No kids. From Minnesota. His friends had also talked him into trying this dating site.

"Eventually, I invited Patrick out to my hometown, and he met my coworkers and my family. Everybody loved him as much as I did. At that point, we started talking about marriage. We had even talked about moving somewhere we could both have a fresh start together. That way neither of us would resent the other for having to give up our families and careers. I was willing to do that for Patrick. I felt that strongly about him."

Abby looked at Jaxon again and saw that he was still listening with that unreadable expression. She almost wished he would show something so she could get a pulse on his thoughts. But, really, in the long run, it didn't matter. His reaction wouldn't change the truth, wouldn't change reality.

"Things started to go south," she continued, staring at the flames. "I thought it was weird that he didn't want me to go to his hometown to meet his family. In fact, I felt a little insulted. He always had a good excuse as to why I couldn't go. But, after a while, it just felt strange. How were we ever going to get married and start a life together if I wasn't allowed to even see where he was from and meet the people that he knew?"

"Good question." Jaxon took a sip of his coffee.

"Eventually, Patrick suggested we should just elope. Though the idea was tempting, I knew it wouldn't be wise. Red flags went up in my mind. One day, Patrick showed up by surprise at my place. But something about him seemed off. I couldn't place what it was exactly, but there was almost a desperation in his eyes.

"After that weekend, I knew I had to call things off with him. I knew it would be better to do it face-to-face, but I also knew I couldn't wait until we saw each other in another month. So I called him. He didn't answer. It was outside of our normal time. We had had a specific schedule because of his work."

Jaxon nodded, letting her know he was listening but nothing else.

Abby continued. "In retrospect I see that it was all just an act, but at the time it made sense. Patrick called me back that evening, and I broke things off with him. He begged me not to. Said that he could make things right, and that he loved me more than anybody he'd ever loved in his life. He sounded very convincing, and, for a moment, I even wondered if I should maybe consider it. But, in the end, I told him that it wasn't a good idea. That we needed space."

Abby attempted to take a sip of her drink. Her words seemed surreal, like she was telling someone else's story. But it had all really happened to her.

"He began to text and email me even more after that. He said that he would do anything to make things work between us. He apologized for not inviting me to meet his coworkers and family and said that he could remedy that if I just gave him some time. I didn't respond initially, because I had asked for space and he clearly wasn't giving it to me.

"About a month later, he showed up again at my door, crying. Begging me to take him back. Something just seemed different about him. He no longer seemed like the man of my dreams or the man that I wanted to marry. In fact, I was having trouble remembering what I'd even seen in him at all. I had to get a couple friends to come over to get him to leave me alone. But eventually he did leave.

"The next week, I happened to be watching TV when I saw the national news come on. I remember the shock that washed over me when I saw Patrick's photo there. He was doing a press conference on his front lawn. His wife had gone missing, and he was begging for the public's assistance in finding her."

CHAPTER SIXTEEN

ABBY WIPED AWAY a tear from beneath her eyes as the memories flooded her. She'd never forget how surreal it had felt to see Patrick at the press confer-ence. It all seemed like a bad dream—but it wasn't.

"Patrick had a whole story worked out," she continued. "He said his wife may have been seeing someone else. It turned out his name really wasn't Patrick Williams, but it was Patrick Finnegan. That's what the ticker said at the bottom of the screen, at least."

"That was the first time you realized that he wasn't who he said he was?" Jaxon asked.

Abby grabbed the blanket from the back of the couch, suddenly chilly. "That's right. Like I said, I began suspecting that something wasn't right, but I had no idea how deeply it went. I just thought he was one of those guys who had presented himself as someone he wasn't on social media. It happens all the time. People put that they're athletic and adventurous when in truth they like watching TV and eating fast food. Everyone tries to make themselves look a little bit better online, right? Either way, I had no clue.

"As soon as I heard what was going on, I called the Minnesota police. I told them who I was and what I knew. It wasn't long after that Patrick became a suspect in his wife's disappearance. Two weeks later, they discovered her dead body in a field about five miles away from their home."

Jaxon shifted, as if he found it hard to stomach that thought. "That's horrible."

"It was definitely horrible. And horrific. Unbelievable. I could go on and on."

"Did they arrest Patrick?"

Abby shook her head. "No, from my understanding, they don't have enough evidence yet."

"But you feel like he's guilty?"

"I do. Even though I tried to help the police, somehow I became the bad guy. The media began to paint me as someone who'd begged Patrick to kill his wife so we could be together." Tears sprung to

Abby's eyes, and she wiped them with her sleeve. "I would never do that. I honestly couldn't even believe anybody would accuse me of doing that. But they had."

"And?" Jaxon stared at her, waiting for Abby to continue.

She sucked in a shaky breath. "I thought it would pass. But then I realized that everyone was looking for some type of sensational story to fuel the gossip chains. They called me 'The Other Woman.' Somehow, despite all the evidence, I became the bad guy. Even people in my hometown began looking at me like I was different. They were wondering if I might have been involved in this woman's murder." Her gaze latched on to Jaxon's. "I promise you, I had nothing to do with what happened. Not that it matters. No one seems to believe me."

Jaxon's face remained expressionless. "And the Executioner?"

She squeezed her eyes shut. "I began getting threats from him shortly after. Honestly, there were so many people who could be responsible for sending those threats. The local police chief didn't seem to take me very seriously. In fact, he acted like I might be complicit with this as well. I felt like I had no choice but to run. That's when I came to Fog

Lake, hoping to lie low until things passed. Mostly, though, I hoped to escape from this man known as the Executioner. That leads me to this moment."

Abby finished. She didn't know what else there was that she could tell Jaxon. Now it was up to him whether or not he was going to believe her.

Jaxon didn't say anything for a minute. Abby had been around enough people to read between the lines. He might want to believe her, but there was always going to be that doubt in his mind now. Whatever goodwill he'd felt toward her was most likely gone.

She stood and wiped her hands on the side of her jeans. "If you don't mind, I think I could use a few minutes to rest and lie down."

Jaxon nodded slowly, almost lethargic. "Help yourself. I'll be down here."

She could feel the disappointment humming from him. Part of her had been drawn to the man, and she'd desperately hoped against hope that he might believe her. That he might be on her side.

But that had been hoping too much.

Hopeless.

There was that word again. It kept wanting to invade Abby's life and her thoughts. She was getting too tired to fight it.

~

AS ABBY DISAPPEARED up the steps, Jaxon leaned back in his chair and let his head fall against the cushions there. That was a lot to comprehend.

Abby had clearly been through a devastating experience, to say the least. Though he could see why some people might wonder if she was guilty, Jaxon's gut told him that she was telling the truth.

Jaxon opened his computer, and out of curiosity Googled Patrick Finnegan's name.

Pages and pages of results came up. This certainly had been a hot news item since Jaxon had started avoiding all media over the past few months. A picture of Patrick stared back at him. The man looked like the all-American boy next door all grown up. He had a charismatic smile, he dressed well, and everybody he worked with had only glowing things to say about him.

Pictured beside him was a blonde woman with an equally big smile. There were various pictures of the couple. One was on the beach, another at a football game, and still another at a Christmas gathering. They certainly looked like a happy couple.

His wife's name was Theresa, and they'd been high school sweethearts. All their friends said they'd seemed happy together and that no one had suspected the two were having problems. Jaxon knew enough about police investigations to know there was probably more to the story yet to be revealed.

Perhaps the police were hanging onto certain pieces of information until the right time. His gaze stopped when he saw a news article that was just released today.

His eyes widened as he read the words there. "It's believed that Abby Brennan was involved as a conspirator in the death of Theresa Finnegan. The police have opened up about some emails that were exchanged between Patrick Finnegan and Brennan. The texts between them detail how they could be together."

Jaxon scanned the emails and felt his muscles tighten until they felt like they might snap. Apparently, based on these emails, Patrick would have to pay so much alimony that he and Abby would never have a decent life together. But if Theresa died, they'd be home free.

Jaxon looked away from his computer and blanched. In all the things that Abby had told him, she'd never mentioned these emails. How could she have been a part of this?

Jaxon forced himself to keep reading. Patrick claimed he refused to go along with what Abby wanted. He also said Abby took matters into her own hands.

Wait . . . he was blaming Abby for the death of his wife? Was that even possible? Jaxon kept reading.

It turned out that the day his wife went missing, Abby had bought a plane ticket out to that area of Minnesota.

He blanched yet again. Another detail that Abby hadn't shared with him. Was that because she was guilty? Jaxon didn't want to believe that was a possibility. Only a few minutes ago, he'd been convinced that she was innocent and had just been dealt a bad hand. But what if that wasn't the case?

He ran a hand over the top of his head and wondered what he should do.

He needed to tell Luke what he had found out. He probably already knew, but just in case he didn't, Jaxon had to share this.

CHAPTER SEVENTEEN

THOUGH ABBY TRIED to lie in bed and rest, there was no chance she would be relaxing. Not with everything that had happened.

She'd been a fool to accept Jaxon's offer of help. Not only did he think she could be guilty, but, if the Executioner did find her, Jaxon would become a target also. She couldn't exploit his kindness. She'd never forgive herself for doing so.

Abby knew without a doubt that she could no longer stay here. She had no idea where she would go or how she would get there. But certainly in this day and age there was another way out of town.

She knew there were no buses here. Jaxon had told her there were no Ubers. Abby couldn't imagine any passenger trains coming through here either.

Abby frowned. Other than hiking or calling someone she knew, there were very few ways for her to get out of town. Besides, Sheriff Wilder had told her she needed to stay in Fog Lake.

She frowned. She didn't want to stay here. Not only did the Executioner know she was in the area, but she was out of resources, and she had no one to trust.

You're a smart girl, Abby. You run your own bakery. You even received some awards for your work. Certainly you can figure out a way to end this.

No good ideas formed in her mind.

Maybe she would ask Jaxon if she could borrow a few bucks, just to get her out of town. Like she'd told him earlier, she didn't like living off charity. She would pay him back.

She stood. It was the only solution she could think of. She had no other choice at this point.

Slowly, Abby made her way downstairs. She paused as she reached Jaxon's door. Before she could knock, Jaxon's voice floated out.

"I think she really might be guilty, Luke . . . that's what all the evidence points to . . . I don't want to believe it either."

Jaxon wasn't going to help her, she realized. She was on her own. She turned and glanced behind her at Fog Lake. If she followed the edge of the lake, it would eventually lead her back into town. Once she was there, maybe she could figure out something.

But what if the Executioner met her on the way?

Fear wracked her body at the thought. But right now she had no other choice.

She had to get out of here.

ABBY COULDN'T STOP GLANCING around her as she followed the edge of the lake. There were sandy stretches of shoreline, followed by rocky areas, followed by parts thick with trees that were difficult to navigate. That wasn't to mention how frigidly cold it was out here. She'd heard somebody in the diner even mention that it might snow today. The air definitely had that feel.

Another tear formed into the corner of her eye. She quickly wiped it away.

She was so tired of crying. She thought she had gotten past that. But everything that had happened here in the past two days had shaken her to her core. This wasn't something that was going to go away. It was something that she was going to have to deal with—and she needed to deal with it head-on.

On one hand, it felt great to get everything off her chest and to bring the truth into the light. On the other hand, seeing the way Jaxon had reacted had been sobering. This was something that she would have to live with for the rest of her life.

Farther down the shoreline, she saw the docks around the harbor area near downtown. If she could just make it there, she could figure out something. Most likely, she would call Renee for help.

Abby didn't want to pull her friend into this, but she had no other choice at this point. She would either borrow someone's cell phone or see if she could find a pay phone. But, one way or another, she had to talk to Renee.

As Abby navigated around another boulder, her blood froze. What was that sound?

Her feet rooted where she stood.

She glanced around but saw no one. She'd seen no one since she started her walk. It was too cold for anyone to be on the water, and most normal people were bundled inside their houses.

Maybe it had just been a squirrel, she rationalized. That made sense.

But she knew the truth. It could have been the Executioner.

What were the chances that he'd already discovered where she was staying?

Abby wanted to think that the chances were slim, but what did she really know?

She was obviously a terrible judge of character. Her head throbbed at the thought. Or was that her heart? She wasn't sure. Maybe it was both.

There the noise was again.

A sound out there didn't fit with her surroundings.

She kept moving but glanced over her shoulder, looking for something to signal where the noise was coming from.

That's when she realized what it was.

Someone was whistling.

Her lungs tightened until she could hardly breathe. It was the same song the Executioner had been whistling when he'd chased her through the woods yesterday. She was sure of it.

Where had she heard it before? Someone she'd known had played or sang it. "Little Red Riding Hood."

The Executioner was here. He'd found her. Now he was going to finish what he had started.

She tried to scream but couldn't.

CHAPTER EIGHTEEN

JAXON HEADED upstairs to Abby's apartment. He still wasn't sure how to react to her or what he was going to say. But Luke needed him to bring her down to the station for more questions. Again.

After all the new facts he'd learned, Jaxon found it hard to think she would be able to stay here. Or that he would be able to act like everything was okay. What Abby had done had been equally as horrific as what Patrick Finnegan had done. She'd played it off so well, never even mentioning why people might suspect her being involved.

He shook his head. Some people were disgusting.

He knocked then stood outside her door and waited. There was no answer and no noise inside.

Irritation snaked up his spine. What was she doing in there?

Jaxon knocked again, faster and louder this time. Again, he waited. And again, there was no sound inside.

His irritation turned into a moment of concern. He grabbed the handle and twisted. The apartment was unlocked.

With a healthy amount of caution, he twisted the knob and pushed the door open. "Abby?"

No answer.

Jaxon scanned the inside of the place. It was small, the only walls being for the bathroom and a small closet. There weren't that many places to hide.

He didn't see Abby anywhere.

He supposed she could be in the shower, but Jaxon didn't think so. She was gone, wasn't she?

Concern squeezed his heart. No matter what happened between them or what the accusations were that had been leveled toward her, she was clearly in danger now and didn't need to be alone. Had she fled out of guilt?

Jaxon didn't know, and it didn't really matter.

Quickly, he checked the bathroom and the closet. Abby was definitely gone. He needed to find her. Not only was she in danger, but Luke needed to talk to her.

After he told Luke what he'd discovered, Luke also told him about a discovery. A body had been found in the woods near Abby's cabin. Whoever this man was that was after her, he wasn't someone to be messed with.

And, in order to find the killer, Jaxon needed to find Abby.

ABBY'S GAZE SWUNG AROUND. Where was he? All she saw was the lake. The woods. Nothing else.

But he was here somewhere. And he was watching.

As she heard the whistle again, fear trickled down her spine. One moment, it sounded like it came from the woods, and the next it sounded like it came from a different direction. The sound echoed over the lake, as if nature played a trick on her.

Abby couldn't just stand here. She had to keep moving.

Her lungs tightened until she could hardly breathe. Images of what the man had threatened to do to her played over and over in her head. If the

Executioner caught her, she was going to experience pain like she had never imagined. Death didn't necessarily scare her, but the process of dying felt terrifying.

She scrambled over some rocks. They were still slippery from this morning's frost. Flakes of icy precipitation floated from the sky and made everything even more slick.

Be careful, Abby. You can't afford to mess up again. No more slips or falls. If you do, next time you might not be so lucky.

Her foot ached where she'd cut it while running barefoot yesterday. The faster she moved, the heavier she breathed and the more her head pulsed.

What had the doctor told her? That she should refrain from doing any vigorous activities?

Abby had little choice right now. She scrambled over another rock and then slid down the other side. As she did, her shoe hit a puddle of water below her, and moisture spread up her jeans.

She shivered as the icy cold lake water shocked her skin.

Again, that was the least of her concerns. She had to keep moving. Her life depended on it.

The whistles were louder. It was almost like the

man moved more quickly toward her. But how could he whistle if he was hustling to catch up with her?

Abby had no idea. But that fact only made his presence even more eerie.

How had he found her? Had he seen her in town and followed her here?

Dear Lord, I know I don't deserve saving, but I'd really love some help right now.

The rocky shore ended, and thick trees formed a blockade in front of her. On the other side, a steep embankment led into the water. Abby was going to have to navigate around the landscape somehow.

Just beyond this obstacle, another cleared shoreline appeared. Was another rental cottage there? She had a feeling it was.

The whistling came from behind her. Abby felt certain. That meant she needed to keep moving forward.

But, as she did, her foot continued to ache and her head to pound.

She was going to have to force herself to move. Otherwise, she was going to die trying to escape. Whatever happened, she was going to fight to the bitter end.

CHAPTER NINETEEN

JAXON STEPPED outside the cabin and scanned everything around him for a sign of where Abby had gone. He saw no indication.

As he hurried to the steps, his gaze homed in on the path stretching from the stairs to the lake.

There were footprints in the soft ground there. Small ones. Prints that could easily belong to Abby.

Had she left and headed toward the lake?

Jaxon followed the steps to the sandy shore around the water. He felt certain that this was the way Abby had gone. It made sense, he supposed. Following the lake would be a more direct path into the town. The road was winding as it twisted along the mountains—not to mention, there was little edge to walk on.

He searched the shoreline, but he couldn't see very much. Fog still covered the area, concealing most of the landscape around him.

Jaxon knew which direction Abby was heading. He also knew the basic layout of the area—knew about each of the houses between his and downtown.

With that in mind, Jaxon hopped into his truck and took off down the road. He would follow the shoreline and stop at various places along the perimeter of the lake to see if he could spot her. Abby couldn't have gotten that far on foot. He still had a chance to catch her.

Most of the houses weren't occupied at this time of the year, so Jaxon didn't foresee any trouble checking them.

His heart throbbed in his ears as he headed down the road. There was a killer out there targeting Abby. He didn't know what role Abby had in the murder of Theresa Finnegan, but he'd like to think she deserved the benefit of the doubt, at least.

He saw the mailbox up ahead and turned onto the gravel lane leading to a cabin by the water. As he suspected, there was no one here. Leaving his keys in the ignition, he hopped out and jogged toward the lake. His gaze scanned everything around him, but he saw no one.

Jaxon really needed this fog to clear so he could see better. But he knew that probably wouldn't be happening anytime soon.

Out of curiosity, he knelt down on the sandy shore.

Footsteps. These matched the ones at his house.

Abby had been here. Now it was just a matter of catching her.

He headed back to his truck and hopped inside. Putting the vehicle into Drive, he continued to follow the lake. The next house was probably a quarter mile away. Maybe—just maybe—Abby had made it that far.

Jaxon reached the next gravel driveway and pulled down it. A massive chalet waited there, again with no cars in the driveway. He hopped out and started toward the shoreline. He needed to let Abby know that he was looking.

He paused on the sandy shores again and glanced to his left then to his right. He hoped and prayed he would spot Abby.

Everything felt eerily quiet and still around him. But he didn't see Abby.

Just as before, he glanced at the ground, looking for those same footprints.

His breath caught when he finally saw them. He knelt down and ran his finger along the shoeprint there.

These were Abby's. She'd been here.

Jaxon lifted his head and looked around. Where was she now? He had a hard time believing she was far away. "Abby?"

No response.

A sound behind him caught his ear.

Was that a stick breaking?

The noise was undercut by another.

Was that a . . . bird?

No, he realized, everything else suddenly feeling dull around him.

Someone was whistling.

Jaxon's muscles tensed.

He should have brought his gun. But he'd left too quickly.

The next instant, he heard someone yell his name. Something hit him, and he collided with the sand just as a gunshot rang out.

~

ABBY HEARD the tires on the gravel and darted behind a tree. She needed just a moment to catch her breath. She knew she didn't have much time.

Every second she wasted gave the Executioner another chance to catch her.

But she'd heard a vehicle arrive. Maybe it was someone who could help her.

Her hands pressed into the tree as the icy air froze her lungs.

Or maybe it was somehow connected with the Executioner.

She didn't know what to think or what the best move was.

Get a grip, Abby. You mess this up, and there are no re-dos. If this guy grabs you, you're a goner.

Then she heard it. Her name.

"Abby!"

Her lungs froze. She knew that voice. Jaxon.

What was he doing here?

As she peered out from behind the tree, another figure appeared in the woods on the other side of the open shoreline. It was a man wearing a blue hat and a blue coat. Just as before, she couldn't make out any other details. She only knew with a startling certainty that he was the Executioner.

He was there. Maybe twenty feet away.

Fear curled around her, squeezing so tightly that Abby couldn't breathe.

The man didn't look at her, though. He was focused on the new voice that came their way.

Jaxon.

The Executioner slipped behind a tree.

Abby's gaze swerved to Jaxon as he walked toward the shoreline, no doubt looking for her.

She fisted her hands until her fingernails cut into her skin. Jaxon shouldn't have come. He should have let her go.

Her eyes went back to the Executioner, but he was gone.

Panic surged through her. Where was he?

That's when she saw him again. Just barely.

He was still behind that tree and probably out of sight from Jaxon, based on the angle where they were standing.

Abby sucked in a breath when she saw something shiny there.

The Executioner had a . . . gun.

A gun? That didn't fit his MO.

But Abby didn't have time to think about that right now.

She saw Jaxon stand from where he'd knelt in

the sand. He'd been tracking her, she realized. She must have left footprints behind. Of course.

Her worst fears were about to be confirmed.

Because of her, Jaxon was now in danger.

The Executioner raised his gun.

Abby had to do something.

Please, Lord. Give me strength now.

Pushing aside her fear, she darted from her hiding place. Running as fast as she could, she headed toward Jaxon. Her foot throbbed with pain, but she ignored it.

First, Jaxon.

She had to get to him before a bullet did. "Jaxon!"

Still three feet away, a burst of energy propelled her. She dove across the sand and tackled Jaxon.

They both hit the ground as the first bullet rang out.

Jaxon looked up at her, his eyes wide and startled. "Abby?"

"You're not safe here." Panic still scrambled through her system.

That man was still out there. He still had a gun. And they were exposed with nothing to protect them.

Jaxon turned so that his body covered hers.

Transforming into the soldier that he was, he looked into the distance. Another gunshot rang out, this time hitting sand beside them.

"We've got to move," Jaxon said.

Before Abby could ask any questions, he took her hand and pulled her toward the trees. "Stay low!"

Just as they reached the patch of woods, another bullet flew through the air. It came close enough that Abby smelled the smoky, acidic scent of the gunpowder.

Jaxon stowed her behind a tree and lingered beside her.

"We've got to get out of here." Jaxon drew in several deep breaths, his adrenaline obviously pumping.

"And how are we going to do that?"

He glanced back toward the chalet. "Very carefully."

The line of trees traveled beside the property. They were going to need to use them as a barrier, Abby realized.

Jaxon took her hand and began pulling her through the woods.

More bullets rang out. Thankfully this guy wasn't a great shot. Abby could be grateful for that, at least.

Finally, they reached the edge of the woods. She saw Jaxon's truck in the driveway, probably eight feet away.

"We're going to have to make a run for it," Jaxon said in her ear. "We'll both get in on my side, and we need to get out of here. There's no time for mistakes."

Abby didn't have the energy to argue, nor did she have any other ideas. She only knew if they stayed here, they'd be dead.

On the count of three, Jaxon pulled her toward his truck. He opened the door, and she dove inside. Jaxon lunged in behind her.

As he jammed the truck into reverse, a bullet shattered the windshield. Pebbles of glass rained down on them, and a cold wind swept inside.

Jaxon pressed the accelerator, and gravel flew up behind them as they took off down the road.

They were both safe. For now. But Abby didn't know how long that would last.

CHAPTER TWENTY

JAXON HADN'T FELT a rush of adrenaline like that since Iraq.

Images from his time there pummeled his thoughts, but he pushed them away. He couldn't afford to lose control right now. He felt certain that the man who had been shooting at them didn't have a vehicle, but they needed to remain on guard. Things could have turned out a lot differently back there.

He glanced at Abby beside him. She was a quivering mess as she wrapped her arms over her chest and stared out the passenger window of the truck.

He wished he had something to offer her—a blanket, a hat even. But he had nothing.

The frigid wind blew across them unobstructed,

and fragments of glass continued to fall in broken bits from the windshield.

But they were alive. That was the important thing.

"Did you get hurt?" He glanced over at her, trying to ascertain her physical state of well-being. He didn't see any blood. That was good. But she had been limping earlier.

"No, I think I'm okay. Just shaken."

His jaw tightened. "You shouldn't have left."

"You shouldn't have come after me." She met his gaze, her voice confident and unwavering.

But he didn't buy it. She'd left because she was terrified. "Why did you leave?"

"I don't want to put you in the middle of this. I didn't want to see the disappointment on your face as you considered that I might be guilty."

"You at least needed to give me time to figure out how I feel. I don't even know what it is yet."

She shook her head, obviously unconvinced still. "You didn't ask to be part of any of this."

"And if you're telling the truth then neither did you."

Abby pressed her lips together but said nothing. They traveled for several moments in silence until she finally asked, "Where are we going?"

"I need to take you to the station."

"Are you turning me in? Because I already told Luke everything that I told you."

Jaxon felt his jaw flex. In his worry, he'd nearly forgotten about that news article he'd found. But he wanted to bring that up when he could look Abby in the eye.

"We need to report what happened, for starters," Jaxon said. "But there's more."

"There's more?" Abby stared at him, almost as if she was trying to read his body language.

They reached the downtown area, and Jaxon found a parking space near the sheriff's office. He put his truck in Park but made no effort to get out. Instead, he let the heat pump out from the vents, trying in vain to fight against the frigid air floating in through the busted windshield.

He kept his irritation in check. But he couldn't handle any more secrets.

"I really wanted to believe that you told me everything," His voice came out lower, more intense than he'd wanted.

But he might as well put it all out there. Holding back would do him no good. He didn't like being tricked, but he needed to hear her side of this.

Abby shook her head, and beads of glass fell into

her lap. "I did tell you everything. What are you talking about?"

"I decided to do a little research while you were upstairs resting. I saw an article containing the emails that you and Patrick exchanged, the ones that show you were involved with his wife's death."

Abby's face visibly paled. "There are no such emails."

"They came out in a magazine article today."

"I'm telling you, those emails don't exist. If someone published them, then the emails were fabricated. I would never do something like that."

"Then what about the plane ticket you bought that put you in Minnesota on the very day Theresa went missing?"

Abby sucked in a deep breath before shaking her head. She rubbed the skin between her eyes.

He'd touched a nerve.

Was this the moment Abby would admit her involvement?

"I did buy that ticket." She raised her head, but her voice sounded almost defeated. "I was going to go out there and confront Patrick, try to put an end to all of this once and for all. At that point, I still didn't even know that he was married."

She drew in a deep breath and released it.

Jaxon waited.

"But I got cold feet," she continued. "I changed my mind, and my best friend, Renee, convinced me that I should just let this go instead of continuing to feed into him by responding whenever he acted out."

Jaxon watched her expression carefully, looking for any sign of deceit. He saw nothing. "So you never got on that plane?"

"That's correct. You can call Renee, and she'll verify what I said. I ended up spending that weekend at her place."

Her body language indicated she was telling the truth. But . . . Jaxon needed to trust but verify. "If you don't mind, I think I will follow up on that."

"Please do."

He turned off his truck and reached for his door handle. "Now we need to get into the station. We need to report what happened, and there's something that Luke wants to tell you."

ANXIETY CONTINUED to rise in Abby as she stepped into the sheriff's office. What now? She had no idea what the sheriff might have to tell her, but she knew without a doubt that it couldn't be good.

In fact, every time she thought this situation couldn't get worse, it did.

At least it was warm in the building. The ride here had been so, so cold that her bones ached. Every time she moved, more shards of glass fell from her hair and shirt. Plus, her foot was killing her and her head still throbbed uncontrollably.

None of that compared to the overpowering fear she felt when she thought about how close she'd come to dying—again.

Sheriff Wilder ushered her and Jaxon into his office and closed the door. He looked tired and still wore his jacket. It appeared he'd just gotten back to the office.

He didn't bother to sit. "We found a body in the woods near your cabin."

Abby's head began to spin. "What?"

Certainly she hadn't heard him correctly. She'd known her cabin was a crime scene. But somehow, she'd convinced herself that maybe it wasn't as bad as she feared. Maybe everything had been staged to look like a murder had happened.

She'd been a fool to even think for a minute that was true.

The sheriff nodded, his neck tight and his gaze suspicious. He pulled a paper from his desk and showed it to her. "Have you ever seen this woman?"

Abby took the photo and studied the image. The woman was probably in her late thirties with dark hair and a pleasant smile. Abby waited for a moment of recognition to hit her, but it didn't.

Abby handed the paper back to him. "I'm sorry, but I've never seen her before. Is this the woman who died?"

The sheriff nodded. "Yes, it is. Her name was Kathy Turner. Her death was . . . brutal, to say the least."

"Her blood matched that in my cabin?" The tones in her voice waivered with stress-born vibrato.

"We'll be testing it, but for now we are assuming that's the case."

Abby closed her eyes, and let her head fall back against the wall. She'd known this man was danger-ous. But she thought that she was his only target. Hearing that the Executioner had gone so far as to brutally murder someone else took this all to a new level.

"Tell Luke what you told me about that plane ticket," Jaxon told her.

Abby looked up at the sheriff and repeated the

story to him. Part of her felt like she was wasting her breath. But Abby couldn't stop telling the truth. She had to stand up for herself. Not give into the hopelessness that wanted to consume her.

"I'm going to want your friend's name and number," he said.

"Of course." Abby rattled the information off to him, and the sheriff jotted it on a paper on his desk.

Sheriff Wilder leaned against his desk, all his attention on her. "I don't know what's going on here, and I don't like it. But I want to find some answers."

"I would love some answers also," Abby said, feeling the first tingle of hope. If their efforts weren't fixated on her, maybe they'd be able to discover the truth.

"Do you have any idea who this man is who sent these threats?"

"No, I have no idea. I assume he's in some way affiliated with Patrick or Theresa. But, for all I know, this could be a random crazy who heard about this online and decided to take action."

The sheriff nodded slowly and tapped his pen on his desk. "Let's see if we can brainstorm some possible suspects. We have a basic description of the man this woman has been seen with in the bar before she disappeared. However, he was sitting in a dark corner, wearing a hat, and an oversized jacket. It doesn't give us much to go on, except that we know he is a white male probably in his late forties with dark hair with a touch of gray."

"That sounds right," Abby said.

The sheriff reached into his desk and pulled out a bottle of water. "You look like you could use some of this."

Abby took it from him and twisted the top off. Her hands trembled as she brought the bottle to her lips and forced herself to take a sip. "What else do you need to know? I want to catch this guy more than anyone."

"Let's talk about some possible suspects. Maybe someone who came here from Minnesota, determined to track you down. I know that, according to what you've told me, you weren't able to meet Patrick's or Theresa's families."

"Not initially," Abby said.

The two men turned toward her.

"What do you mean?" Jaxon asked, disbelief in his voice.

"I mean that, before all this came out, I had never met them. But once the news hit the media, Theresa's uncle paid me a visit."

"Does Theresa's uncle fit the description of the man who's been following you?" Jaxon asked.

Abby shrugged. "I've thought about it dozens of times myself, and I really don't know. Her uncle's name was Marshall, and he was definitely an outdoorsman. But I didn't talk to him enough to really get that much more information on him."

"Why did he come to see you?" the sheriff asked.

The moment flashed into her mind. "He thought that I was responsible for his niece's death, and he came out to Georgia—that's where I'm really from—to give me a piece of his mind."

The sheriff crossed his fingers together, his intense gaze still on her. "So I'm assuming he was angry."

"You're assuming correctly." Abby rubbed the side of her water bottle, as blips of that conversation flooded back to her.

"Honestly, he showed up at my house early in the morning. I had no idea who he was when I opened the door. I could only tell that he was upset."

"What happened next?" Sheriff Wilder asked.

"He asked me how I could possibly live with myself. He was so angry. I didn't know what to do or what to say, and I could feel myself getting worked up. I could feel the tears coming on. He wasn't listening. He hadn't come to hear my side of things. He only came to make me feel bad. Eventually, I shut the door, pulled the shades, and turned off my phone. He stayed outside my house for another hour or so."

"Did you ever tell the police?" the sheriff asked.

"No, at that point, I didn't feel like they would do anything. The police chief . . . his wife ran against my stepmom for city council and lost. He hasn't liked me since then. But I promise, if I had known for one moment that Patrick was married . . . I would've never ever dated him. But he pulled the wool over my eyes. I saw no indications that he was anyone other than the person he presented himself to be. At least, at first. As soon as I began to doubt the story, I called things off."

The sheriff had to believe her. Abby may have withheld information earlier, but she hadn't made any of this up. Her words were true.

Someone knocked at the door, and Abby looked up to see the receptionist standing there. "Bill Murdoch is here to see you."

The sheriff nodded before turning to Abby. "He's the man who found the body while he was out hunting."

Her throat tightened as she imagined it playing out.

"Don't try to run again." The sheriff stood, locking gazes with her. "Not only is it not safe, but I need you here for more questions. Do you understand?"

"I do."

Rising, Jaxon touched her elbow and led her out into the lobby. As he did, she glanced over at the man waiting there.

Fifties. Tall. Average build. Beard.

She sucked in a breath as fear raked through her.

No, that man wasn't the Executioner.

He was the one who'd found the dead body in the woods.

So why did seeing him cause Abby's body to revolt? To want to hurl again?

How had this Bill Murdoch found the woman?

Was it because he'd been the one to kill her?

Abby's head swirled at the thought.

CHAPTER TWENTY-ONE

JAXON'S THOUGHTS raced as they headed back to his cabin. None of this seemed real. Instead, it seemed like a nightmare that he'd stepped into. If he felt this way, he could only imagine Abby's emotions.

Just as before, a cool wind hit their faces from the shattered windshield. The frigid air shocked Jaxon's senses. Icy precipitation occasionally mingled with the air as it rushed over their skin and through their hair.

If he could see through the darkness, he'd see remnants of the fire that had scorched this area not even a year ago. The area was starting to recover, but the foliage would take time to repair itself. That was because repair and healing took time, not only for the forest but for people too.

"Where are we going?" Abby's voice broke Jaxon from his thoughts. She nearly had to shout to be heard over the air rushing inside his truck.

"Back to my cabin."

She sucked in a quick breath. "But is that even safe?"

"Is anywhere really safe?"

The question seemed to shake her up, and Abby pulled her arms more tightly over her chest. "I suppose not."

"At my place, at least I know how to defend myself. I'm familiar with all the creaks and all the various ways to get in. Plus, that's where my gun is."

"I totally understand if you no longer want me to stay there."

"Where else would you go?"

Abby shook her head, an almost hollow look in her eyes. "Truthfully? I have no idea. I thought I was a planner. I've always been the type to have a savings account and a backup emergency fund. I buy every insurance that's out there. But there are some things that you just can't prepare for. This was one of them."

Jaxon could appreciate her honesty. If what Abby was telling him was the truth, then she really was in a tough, tough spot—to say the least.

Darkness surrounded them, along with fog and dark skeletal trees. The cold air rushing in from the windshield did nothing to help the situation. He would have to take his truck in to have it fixed, but he had other bigger issues at hand now.

When they got back to his cabin, Jaxon stepped out of his truck and glanced around. His muscles tightened in anticipation of possible trouble.

He saw and heard nothing out of the ordinary. But that didn't mean that the man wasn't out there, waiting for them right now.

He hurried around to Abby's side of the truck and opened her door. Still on guard, he took her arm and led her into the cabin. "Stay here while I check the rest of the place."

She didn't argue.

He checked out his cabin, and it was clear.

With all the doors locked and doublechecked, and his gun tucked into his waistband, Jaxon returned to Abby. She stood near the wall where he'd left her, still looking entirely too pale for his comfort. She'd been through a lot today—for the past month, according to all she'd shared.

There was something Jaxon needed to say to her —something he should have said sooner.

He paused in front of her, his heart seeming to

catch in his throat. "Look, thank you for what you did back there at the lake. You saved my life."

Abby shrugged as if it wasn't a big deal. "Maybe we're even now. However, you wouldn't be in danger right now if it wasn't for me."

He saw all her emotions—the guilt, the sorrow, the apology.

Lowering his voice, he said, "I think it's safe to say that you don't have any control over that."

Even though Jaxon wanted to question whether or not Abby was complicit in any of this, the fact that she'd put her own life on the line to save his spoke volumes. How could he doubt her after that? But there was still so much he didn't know.

Jaxon was anxious to hear what Abby's friend Renee told Luke. Once Abby had a solid alibi for Theresa's murder, he could finally rest assured that Abby was innocent in all this.

But then there were those emails . . . had they really been forged? It seemed so extreme. Then again, so did murder.

The facts all collided inside his head, begging to be sorted out.

He fixed them some coffee, and he and Abby sat on the couch together. He cut to the chase. "How could someone forge those emails?"

"I don't know." Abby shook her head. "Can I see them? I don't even know what they say."

He grabbed his laptop from the end table, pulled up the article, and handed the computer to her. Abby's eyes widened before she finally squeezed them shut.

"I am not a tech genius, but Patrick is," she murmured. "That's what he does for a living. Is it possible that he could have somehow tapped into my IP address and created these emails?"

"I suppose anything is possible. But why would he try to set you up like this?"

She rubbed the side of her coffee mug. "When all this came out and I tried to break things off with him, he threatened me. He told me that if I broke up with him, he was going to make my life miserable. I thought he was just speaking out of hurt and anger. Maybe he set me up to take the fall."

"But if he loved you so much, why would he do that?" Jaxon didn't really expect Abby to have an answer. But the question remained in his mind.

"You know that saying, if I can't have you no one else can? Maybe this fits into that also. Patrick was obsessive and desperate. I didn't see it until the very end. But someone who's willing to kill their spouse in order to be with me?" Abby shook her head and pulled her sleeves over her hands. "There's no telling what else he would do."

"Do you think Patrick is the Executioner?"

She remained silent before shaking her head. "I suppose it could be a possibility, but Patrick is in his early thirties."

"Could this man be wearing a disguise of some sort?" Jaxon had seen stranger things before. Most people's observation skills weren't as strong as they'd like to believe.

"I suppose that's a possibility," Abby said after a moment of thought.

"There's nobody else you can think of who might be responsible?"

Abby let out a long breath, her gaze appearing fragile and distant. "I did read some articles on Theresa after all this came out. I know that a lot of people in her family were avid outdoorsmen. That doesn't mean they're guilty, but I do feel like whoever is behind this knows his way around the forest. This man . . . he's not nervous. He seems to know exactly what he's doing."

"He wasn't exactly a great shot today . . . thank goodness." Things would be a lot different right now if the man had been. Jaxon hadn't even realized the man was close, and he considered his instincts to be finely tuned. They'd kept him—along with his men—alive on the battlefield.

"You're right, he wasn't. I suppose there are hunters who are bad shots but who still enjoy the sport." Abby shifted, pulling her legs closer to her. "I've had way too much time on my hands to think about the details of this. It's almost been an obsession. That said, I still have no idea who might be behind this. I've come up with nothing, no one."

Jaxon reached forward, squeezed her hand, and then released it. "We're going to figure out what happened here. Luke is a great detective. I know he seems intense when he's dealing with you, but he's a really good guy who genuinely cares about people."

Abby looked down at her hand—to the area Jaxon had touched. She rubbed it.

Was she trying to erase the feel of her skin against his?

Maybe he'd overstepped.

Finally, she tucked her hand under her leg and said, "I believe it. I know it's a tough position that the sheriff is in right now."

"I say we just lie low here for tonight and see what tomorrow has to bring."

"That sounds like a great idea." As her gaze went back to the computer screen, she sucked in a breath. "Jaxon, there's another article about me—one that tells the world I'm here in Fog Lake hiding out."

Jaxon's muscles clenched. Someone in town had seen Abby and leaked that information. He prayed that more trouble didn't come their way.

ABBY STARED across the couch at Jaxon. He had released her hand, and she thought it was kind that he'd even attempted to bring some comfort to her, especially considering everything that had happened.

As soon as he pulled his hand back into his lap, she missed his touch. She craved the brief moment of comfort he'd offered.

Questions swirled in her head. At this point, she felt she didn't have anything left to lose by asking them.

"You know a lot about me, Jaxon," Abby started. "But I hardly know anything about you."

His gaze met hers, an unreadable expression there. "What do you want to know?"

"What happened to change things between you

and your siblings?" Abby pulled a leg beneath her and watched Jaxon.

His eyes widened with surprise. "What do you mean?"

"I know it's none of my business, but there's obviously some tension between you and the rest of your family. I just can't figure out why. You all seem so close."

His jaw flexed, and Abby was sure he wasn't going to share any details. She probably *shouldn't* have asked. But, for some reason, she had the burning desire to know.

Just when she thought Jaxon wasn't going to respond, he let out a deep breath and said, "When I was barely a teenager, my dad was diagnosed with cancer," Jaxon started. "When my mom found out, she ran away with another man here in town. When my dad needed her the most—when the family needed her the most—she hit the road."

"I'm sorry."

"My siblings were furious with her, and, for a while, so was I. But she's still my mom, and, despite what she'd done, I didn't want to end things with her. I began communicating with her without my siblings' knowledge."

Facts began clicking in place in Abby's mind. "Do they know now?"

"To my knowledge, they don't. It's not that I want to keep secrets. I just want to avoid the drama of it. I totally understand where they're coming from. I know they'll feel betrayed when they find out. But you only get one mom in this life. I knew I had to forgive her. The anger would eat me up inside otherwise."

The muted tone of his voice made Abby's heart twist with compassion. "I think that makes you the bigger person."

Jaxon shrugged, his gaze fixated on the flames in the fireplace. "I don't know about that. I just know that there are a lot of things in my life that I need forgiveness for, so who am I to hold it back from somebody else?"

Abby tilted her head, trying to convey her gratitude toward Jaxon for sharing this part of his life with her. His words contained so much wisdom. "So you still meet with her?"

His gaze broke from the fire, and he took a sip of his coffee. "For a long time, while I was stationed overseas, it was only emails and texts. But since I came back to this area, we've been having a weekly lunch date. It's been good to keep up with her."

"Why did you get out of the military? You seem like one of those guys who would want to be in for life."

"I thought I did. But all that changed with my last mission in Iraq."

Something cold washed over Abby. Just hearing the mellow tone in his voice brought Abby chills, even though she hadn't heard any details yet. She didn't ask, even though she wanted to know. If Jaxon wanted to share, then he would.

"My men and I had been assigned to guard a terrorist leader who was giving intel to the US in exchange for his freedom. The man was vile. It wasn't a job that I wanted to do, but when you're in the military, you do what you're told to do."

"What happened?" Abby's mind raced as she tried to put together what he'd gone through. She pulled a pillow on her lap and waited.

"One day while I was guarding the perimeter of the compound, the man's wife came out. She begged me to help her. When she held up her arms, her sleeves slipped down, and I saw the bruises there. I knew that she was in a dire situation."

Abby let out a little gasp. Though she knew how women were sometimes treated in those countries, hearing about it firsthand was still shocking.

Jaxon continued. "I didn't know what to do. I had been given orders, and I knew that she'd taken a huge risk by even coming out to find me. Initially, I told her that I couldn't help. I tried to put her out of my mind and focus on my job. But, every week, she would find me. Sometimes she didn't have to say a word. It was just a glance that she gave me as she walked past."

"So what happened?"

"I finally decided I was going to risk it all to save her. I figured out a way I could sneak her onto one of our trucks as they were leaving the compound. It was risky. I could've lost my job. Everything was on the line. But I knew it was the right thing to do. Especially after I saw her holding her side one day. She told me that she'd dropped a plate of food, and her husband had beat her."

"That's terrible." Abby couldn't imagine living like that.

Yet she could.

She knew all too well about living in fear for her life. Still, her situation felt different.

"On the day before she was supposed to escape, her husband caught wind of what was going to happen. He was furious. I was outside the compound when I heard Nailah scream. I rushed inside, but I was too late." His voice cracked. "She was dead. He'd beaten her to death."

Abby's hand covered her mouth in horror. "So what did you do?"

"I started to go after him, but one of my men pulled me back before I did something I'd regret. I'm not actually sure I would've regretted it, but it could have ruined the deal the US had with this man. And, in that country, what that man had done wasn't a crime. It was an honor killing. It still burns me up to think about it." Jaxon fisted his hands beside him, as if fighting unseen emotions.

"Did anything ever happen to this man?"

"Last I heard, he's still an informant for the US. After that, I knew I had to get out. I couldn't put myself in those situations again. But every day I live with the fact that I could've helped her."

Abby wanted more than anything to reach out and squeeze his arm, to offer some kind of comfort. But Jaxon was too far away, and they didn't have that kind of relationship . . . did they? They seemed to quickly be growing close. The thought both thrilled and terrified her.

"You were going to help her," Abby said.

"But I was too late. I should've helped her sooner."

Abby opened her mouth, about to say more. Before she could, a sound floated into the house.

Someone was whistling.

The blood left Abby's face.

The *Executioner* was whistling.

He was here.

CHAPTER TWENTY-TWO

JAXON BRISTLED as he rose to his feet. The Executioner was here. Outside the cabin. Taunting them.

Jaxon grabbed his gun and tucked it into his waistband. "Abby, get in the closet and close the door. Don't come out for anyone but me."

Abby reached for him, her eyes wide with fear. "But Jaxon . . ."

"I can handle it myself."

Jaxon didn't tell Abby, but she was his second chance. She was his opportunity to make things right and to not let another maniac claim an innocent life.

"He's trying to lure you out." Desperation crept into Abby's voice as she clung to his arm.

"I can handle myself."

"Jaxon . . ."

"Go in the closet. Please."

Abby stared at him a moment longer before nodding. She scrambled across the room and slipped behind the door and into the space where Jaxon had found her that day she'd thought the Executioner was outside. Jaxon waited until the door closed before he grabbed his gun and stepped onto the porch.

All his senses felt alive as he glanced around him at the darkness.

The whistling still floated through the air. The man was out there somewhere. But what was this guy's game plan? Why had he come here, and what was he hoping to prove?

Jaxon couldn't make himself an easy target by just standing here. Instead, he stepped into the shadows and gripped his Glock. Was the man planning to shoot him? He obviously had a gun.

If that was the case, he could've done it as soon as Jaxon stepped onto the front porch. But he hadn't. That led Jaxon to believe the Executioner didn't plan on killing him that way. Not today, at least.

Slowly, Jaxon crept forward, dry leaves crinkling

under his boots as he followed the sound of the whistling.

What was that tune? "Little Red Riding Hood" maybe?

Jaxon had heard the song when he was younger. He'd found it haunting back then, but right now he found it even more so.

Did this man think that Abby was a Little Red Riding Hood? Did he consider himself the Big Bad Wolf? The picture of this man being a hunter and Abby being a victim made his stomach roil.

Using all the stealth inside him, he maneuvered through the trees. The one advantage Jaxon had was that he knew this area and these grounds.

The noise stopped, and Jaxon froze. He couldn't give away his location. He had to be careful here because he had no idea what this man was thinking, and he didn't want to walk into a trap.

The hairs on Jaxon's arms rose as everything grew eerily silent around him. Even the wind had died down, and nature seemed motionless as it anticipated what would happen next.

Still nothing.

Jaxon took a few more steps, remaining on guard.

He paused when he saw something in the

distance. Was that a . . . person? Just standing there against the tree?

Carefully, he crept closer.

The person didn't move. No, they were eerily still.

Jaxon's instincts told him to remain cautious.

As he reached the figure, Jaxon grabbed the person's shoulder.

But it wasn't a person.

It was . . . a jacket?

As the garment draped in his hand, he saw a tear on the back. It must have been nailed to a tree.

After glancing around once more, Jaxon examined the clothing more closely.

It was definitely a jacket. A blazer. Like one that a woman would wear.

Jaxon sucked in a breath at what he saw on it.

Blood. Lots of blood.

This had to be from the woman who'd been killed.

The Executioner had left it here to send a message. Nausea roiled in his stomach.

Jaxon had to call Luke.

Now.

~

ABBY LEANED into the wall of the closet, wishing she could disappear. Wishing she was out there fighting her own battles. Thankful that she was safe.

Her emotions were all over the place as she waited.

What was going on out there? Was Jaxon okay?

She prayed he was.

She continued to wait. Her heart thumped in her ears as she strained to hear any telltale signs of what was going on.

Finally, she heard footsteps coming her way.

Was it Jaxon? Or the Executioner?

Panic swelled in her until she felt she could hardly breathe.

The next instant, the door flew open and light flooded inside.

She blinked against the brightness and raised her hands, ready to defend herself.

Instead . . . Jaxon stood there.

"You okay?" His eyes narrowed as he observed her.

It took every ounce of her energy not to crumple right there. Instead, she stepped out and nodded. "You?"

He told her what had happened, and the sickly

feeling in her gut continued to grow stronger, more potent with each new detail.

A few minutes later, Luke came and took their statements, as well as collected the evidence. The ritual was becoming a routine around here.

When the sheriff left, silence slipped between Jaxon and Abby. What a day.

Jaxon wandered over to the window and shoved aside the curtain. Quietly, Abby joined him. She gave him time to process his thoughts. She was still processing hers.

A moment later, Jaxon nodded toward the lake. "When I was a kid, my dad took me out here to look at the fog on the lake."

She followed his gaze and saw that eerie haze over the water. "Is that right?"

"My dad loved being outside more than anything."

"I guess you got that from him?"

"Really, all of us kids did. He'd take us camping and tell us stories about this town's history. When I used to see the fog coming off the lake, I used to think the fog was actually the souls of people who'd been massacred here."

Abby shivered at the imagery. "That's a beautiful

yet eerie image. I can see why a child might think that."

His jaw flexed as he continued to stare out the window. "The thing about this area is it always reminds me that hope can rise from destruction. We can't change the past. We can't change what happened. But we can make the best of things and change the future instead."

"I love that, Jaxon."

His words echoed in her mind. *We can't change the past . . . but we can change the future instead.*

Those were words she was going to hold onto also.

Maybe all hope wasn't lost.

CHAPTER TWENTY-THREE

I STOOD NEAR THE LAKE. Its frosty claws seemed to spread over everything until the cold ripped into my skin.

I'd liked this town at first, but I liked it less and less all the time. It shouldn't take me so long to do what I needed to do. I never anticipated people actually being on Abi-jail's side.

Especially not Jaxon Wilder.

I smiled. Yes, I knew his name. Of course. I knew how to find out the information I needed. My brilliance was so often underestimated.

I knew Jaxon had been in Iraq. He was decorated for his heroism. I also knew about his shaky family life and the secret he held from his siblings.

I pulled my hat down lower and let out a little *tsk tsk*. People shouldn't keep secrets from their family. My family certainly hadn't kept secrets, and I would hold them up to anyone right now.

I'd gone to his place to taunt him this evening, and I might go back later. Whatever I could do to get in Jaxon's head. To send messages. To let people know who was in control.

Me, of course.

I shoved my hands down into my pockets and let the nighttime work for me, concealing my presence. Nature knew what I needed and complied with my wishes. That's why I was staying in the woods. Off a little road where the trees could protect me. It worked perfectly for what I needed it for.

By now, people in this town were keeping an eye open for me. It wasn't my fault. But, last night, I'd had to do what I had to do.

My muscles tightened as I thought about it.

That woman had come on to me. She was impure and willing to do things that no single woman should be willing to do. I'd tried to put her in her place, but she wouldn't listen. Instead, she'd gotten offended. Then she stopped respecting me.

That was when I knew I had to take action.

Because no one disrespected me—especially not floozies like that brunette.

The rage inside me had surprised even me. It felt so good to get my frustrations out. Someone had to pay, and I was the one who wanted to make a statement.

People needed to act like they had virtues. Especially women. They'd grown accustomed to using their feminine charms to get what they wanted, not caring who might be hurt in the process.

I fisted my hands as I thought about it. Stay calm, I told myself. In control. I sucked in a deep breath and then another and another.

As I did, a car pulled up to the lake. I watched carefully and saw a man and woman inside. They were too old to be teenagers. If I had to guess, based on the make of the car and the out-of-state license plate, they were here with one of the corporate getaways.

Those people. Snooty. Privileged. Thought they were better than everyone else. I couldn't stand them.

My gaze went back to the car that had pulled into the little gravel lot off the beaten path. I imagined this was probably a pretty popular spot for couples to get away and get frisky. There had been a few spots like this in the area where I'd grown up also. I knew all about them.

I remained in the shadows and watched.

I'd seen that woman earlier talking with some of her girlfriends while they were in a local coffee shop. She'd mentioned her husband back home.

But the man she kissed right now was not her husband.

A new round of anger built up in me until I felt like a volcano that was about to erupt.

Why did people think they could act like this? It boggled my mind.

The items on my to-do list seemed to grow. First, I needed to get Jaxon Wilder out of the way. He needed to pay—but not in the way that Abby Brennan needed to pay. She needed to suffer. Jaxon, on the other hand, just needed to disappear.

I looked back at the car. It looked like another task had been handed to me. These things seemed to drop in my lap, these situations that needed to be handled.

Justice needed to be quick, and it needed to be obvious.

This woman was doing something she should not be doing.

It was a good thing I was patient. I would wait. At the right opportunity, I would give her the chance to repent. If she didn't, she'd have to pay the price.

And I would enjoy every minute of it.

At the thought of it, I began whistling again.

CHAPTER TWENTY-FOUR

JAXON WOKE up early the next morning—if he'd even call it waking up. He'd hardly gotten any sleep last night as he'd waited to hear someone outside his house. He'd been on guard, ready to spring into action if necessary.

To be on the safe side, Jaxon had decided to sleep on the couch and let Abby have his room. He felt better knowing that she was close. The upstairs apartment had its own entrance and felt too secluded right now.

After he started the coffee pot, Jaxon paced over to his bedroom doorway. It was cracked. Pushing aside any guilt at invading Abby's privacy, Jaxon peered inside. Abby's sleeping figure lay in his bed. The sound of her breathing offered proof of life.

He looked away. Good. She was okay. That was all he needed to know.

More at ease, he went to his front door and stepped outside. A bitterly cold wind greeted him and a light layer of snow had been left on his doorstep.

Normally, Jaxon loved this time of year in the mountains. There was nothing like seeing the glistening white slopes. But, right now, he wasn't in the position to enjoy anything. He just wanted to get to the bottom of what was going on with Abby.

Before he stepped back inside, something in the dusting of snow caught his eye. There, on the wooden planks of his deck. Were those . . .?

Footprints. They were definitely footprints, and large ones at that.

Jaxon bristled and reached for the gun in his waistband. He scanned the area around him. His driveway. The woods. The lake.

Was the man here right now?

Jaxon saw nothing out of the ordinary. Saw no one. Heard only silence.

But that didn't mean he was safe.

Carefully, he followed the footprints around the perimeter of the cabin and saw that the tracks stopped at each window.

The Executioner had been here last night. He'd come and peered inside, probably trying to see if Abby was here or not. Thank goodness, they'd pulled all the curtains and shades shut.

But Jaxon didn't like this. How could he not have heard the man on his porch?

Unless the man was stealthy, just as Abby had said. Maybe he hadn't wanted Jaxon to hear. Maybe he hadn't even wanted to get inside. Maybe he had just wanted to send a message. Jaxon's muscles tightened at the thought.

With one last glance around his property, Jaxon went back inside and locked the door again. He slipped his gun back into his waistband, but his muscles felt poised to grab it at the first indication he would need it.

He glanced at his watch. It was already eight o'clock. Certainly, Luke was at the station by now. Good. Because Jaxon wanted to talk with him.

He dialed his brother's number, and Luke answered on the first ring. Something about his voice made him sound tired, indicated he hadn't gotten much sleep again last night. Jaxon didn't envy his brother's job.

"You don't sound too hot." Jaxon still watched the front door, almost as if his subconscious expected the Executioner to show up at any minute.

"I'm not. It was another long night."

Jaxon's back muscles tensed, and he poured some coffee. "Did something else happen?"

"Another woman is missing."

Jaxon sucked in a breath. Certainly he hadn't heard correctly. "What?"

"Her name is Marissa Wilcox. She's twenty-seven. From Virginia. Here on a corporate retreat. She never came back to her hotel last night. According to her roommate, she went to meet someone and never returned. We found her car in a lot near the lake, but she's nowhere to be seen."

His heart pounded in his ears. "Any blood?"

"No, not this time. But we're pulling the dogs out, hoping we can track her."

Jaxon set his coffee down on the table. "Do you think it's the same guy?"

"If I had to bet on it, I'd say yes. I'm not sure how he's targeting his victims, but I do know that this woman was last seen with one of her coworkers."

"Okay . . ." Jaxon sensed there was something his brother wasn't saying.

"Her coworker was a man, and she's married to somebody else."

Realization spread through Jaxon. The Judge, Jury, and Executioner suddenly made more sense. This man had deemed himself a moral authority and was punishing those he saw as sinners.

"I see," Jaxon finally said.

"Is that why you were calling?"

Jaxon told him about the footprints on his porch.

"So you think this guy was at your place again last night?" Luke asked.

"That's my guess. I don't know what his game plan is, but I don't like it."

"I don't like it either."

"Listen, did you call Abby's friend Renee?" Jaxon was anxious to hear confirmation on Abby's story. Anxious to know the truth. To quell his doubts.

"I tried to last night, but neither she nor her husband answered."

More unease sloshed inside of Jaxon. "I see."

"I'll let you know when I hear from her. We're still looking for other similar cases throughout the country—starting in Minnesota. Nothing yet. In the meantime, be careful."

"I will."

"Do you want me to send a deputy to sit outside the house?"

"No, not yet," Jaxon said. "I'll let you know if I change my mind."

"I'll send someone over to take some pictures. And, I know this is bad timing, but don't forget, Harper's birthday party this evening."

"Is it still on?"

"She deserves to be celebrated," Luke said. "I want to do everything I can to make it happen. Do you think you can still make it?"

"I wouldn't miss it for the world."

THE SCENT of coffee jostled Abby from her sleep. She'd rested surprisingly well considering everything that had happened. It had nothing to do with the leather scent of Jaxon that seemed to permeate his room.

That thought was ridiculous. Sure, the man was handsome and chivalrous, but that didn't mean Abby was attracted to him. Still, she couldn't deny she found something very comforting about his presence.

She pushed herself up in bed. What would today bring? Did she really even want to know?

Sometimes, Abby thought she didn't. Sometimes

it would be nice just to freeze this very moment, this instant where nothing else had gone wrong. She knew when she got out of bed, she would face more problems, more questions, and probably more danger.

Maybe she should leave. Get out of town. Leave this area behind.

Then she remembered Luke's words to her—that she had to stay here because of the investigation.

She ran a hand through her hair. She just needed to get ready. To stop sitting here thinking things over again and again.

Twenty minutes later, when she stepped out into the living room, she saw a cup of coffee waiting for her on the counter. Jaxon sat on the sofa, looking at his computer screen.

She sucked in a breath. The man was a sight to behold.

The fire blazed behind him and a light dusting of snow feathered the windowpanes. His red-and-black flannel shirt nicely displayed his muscles. But it was his eyes that got to her. They showed his kind yet honorable soul.

Abby picked up the coffee and sat across from him. "Morning."

He closed the laptop and offered a quick smile.

"Good morning."

"Thanks for the coffee." She held it beneath her nose. "It smells great."

Jaxon's eyes lit as he turned toward her. "Good news. I just found out that somebody requested a coffee order for a shop in Gatlinburg."

"That's great news. I didn't know that you were shopping it around."

"I wasn't shopping it around, but my two sisters-in-law decided to take matters into their own hands."

Abby smiled. "They sound like smart women."

He shrugged good-naturedly. "I like them."

"So what does this mean for you?" Abby pulled a blanket around her legs, trying to ward away the morning chill.

"The buyer wants to come out tomorrow to talk to me."

"I am really happy for you, Jaxon. Maybe you have found your new calling in life."

He offered a boyish shrug again.

As soon as his laid-back response disappeared, he straightened. "Listen, Abby, there's something I need to tell you. Another woman has gone missing."

The blood drained from Abby's face. Certainly she hadn't heard him correctly. "What?"

"I just talked to Luke about thirty minutes ago. They're still looking for her."

She shook her head, wishing this was all a nightmare. But it wasn't, was it? The danger around her grew more serious by the moment. Nothing she did could stop that. "Why does this guy keep doing this? I just don't understand it."

"If he's doing it here, there's a good chance he's done it somewhere else. Luke is looking into other similar cases outside this area right now. I just wanted you to know that."

Abby nodded and ran a hand through her hair. "I appreciate the update. I wonder if he ever talked to Renee."

"I asked him, and he said he hasn't been able to get up with her yet."

"She usually has that phone attached to her. Then again, who knows what she has going on right now." Abby tried to keep the worry out of her voice.

She knew that danger didn't encompass every area of her life, but her mind was programmed to think the worst at this point. Certainly, the lack of communication was a coincidence. In an hour or two, Renee would call the sheriff back, and everyone would know Abby couldn't have killed Theresa Finnegan.

Abby craved that vindication, that validation. She needed people to know she would never hurt someone else, especially out of spite.

She cleared her throat, trying to push her grim thoughts aside as she turned back to Jaxon. "Do you have anything on your agenda today? I don't want to keep you from anything."

"Actually, I was just going to roast a little more coffee," Jaxon said. "Tonight is Harper's birthday party. You can come."

"I hate to intrude."

"You're not intruding. I'm inviting you."

Abby stared at him. Jaxon seemed sincere. And if she didn't go, she knew Jaxon wasn't going to leave her alone. He'd miss the party first.

Finally, she nodded. "Okay, then. The least I can do is to make some cookies."

"Let's see what I have."

Abby nodded. She wanted to pretend that today would be happy and normal. But she knew that wouldn't be the case—not with the Executioner still out there. Still, maybe just for a little while she could forget her troubles.

Yet she had no doubt they would still be there, waiting to pounce at the first opportunity.

CHAPTER TWENTY-FIVE

TWO HOURS LATER, Abby glanced at one of her sweet creations as they cooled on the kitchen counter.

She and Jaxon had a surprisingly great time baking together. Michael Bublé played on some Bluetooth speakers, the scent of vanilla floated in the area, and a light snow had begun falling outside.

Jaxon had shown her how he took raw coffee beans and roasted them there in his kitchen. He'd have to invest in some larger roasters if he ever decided to make a business out of his coffee. The whole process was fascinating.

Jaxon nodded at Abby's cookies. "They look really great."

"Decorating is my specialty." She held up a sugar

cookie that had been expertly iced to look like a birthday cake. "I know I told you that I worked in a restaurant, but I don't. I'm sorry I didn't tell the truth. I actually own a bakery called Sprinkles."

"I like that name." Jaxon nodded as if he were impressed. "It looks like you obviously have the talent for doing this kind of thing."

"It's what I've always loved doing. However, after everything that happened, I had to shut it down. Messages were being spray-painted on my front windows. The glass door was broken once. People were trying to organize boycotts. It got really ugly." Her hand trembled, causing the icing to veer off the side of the cookie. Abby paused and shook her head at her mistake.

"It's sad what people do when they feel like they're threatened, isn't it?"

"You hit the nail on the head. That's what it boils down to. People think that I'm guilty, and they think that if they can punish me for what I supposedly did, that it will make a statement. But, the fact is, I didn't do the things that they're accusing me of doing." Ignoring the tension in her shoulders, she used a toothpick to clean up the edge of the cookie. Too bad it wasn't that easy to clean up the mistakes made in life.

"I'm sorry you're having to go through all this." Jaxon's hand came down softly on her shoulder.

"Me too." Her frown disappeared, and she sucked in a deep breath, trying to compose herself. Finally, she held up a cookie. "Here you go. Try one."

Jaxon took a bite. The buttery sweetness of the cookie washed over his senses, and he nodded in approval. "This is really good."

Abby grinned. "Thank you."

"Your cookies and my coffee . . . they could make a good team, I think."

"Maybe they could."

For a moment, Abby forgot that her life was back in Georgia. The only thing that really tied her to the area was her best friend, Renee. Sure, her dad was there, but Abby had been so utterly disappointed in his reaction over what had happened, that Abby feared it would drive a wedge between them.

The two of them had never been particularly close, especially after her mother died. He'd recently gotten remarried and now had a new insta-family that he showered all his time and attention on.

In fact, maybe that's why he seemed so upset over the accusations leveled against Abby. It painted his new family in a bad light. His wife didn't like the bad press that came with the accusations.

Abby had so much fun baking this morning, she'd almost forgotten about everything else that was going on in her life. But she couldn't afford to do that. Instead, she needed to wait—to prepare—for the next shoe to drop.

A knock sounded at the door. Jaxon instantly tensed and put his cookie down, all signs of the fun they'd been having gone.

"Stay here." Jaxon withdrew his gun and paced to the door.

Abby held her breath, waiting to see who was going to be on the other side.

JAXON PAUSED as a voice sounded on the other side of the door. "Jaxon, it's me. Luke. Open up."

He released his breath and put his gun back into his waistband before opening the door. His brother stood on the porch, along with a deputy.

"We stopped by to check out those footprints," Luke said.

"Come on in." Jaxon stepped aside to let Luke in.

"My deputy is going to take pictures." Luke stomped some of the snow from his feet on the mat there before closing the door.

He nodded at Abby, who was still decorating in the kitchen.

Flour dusted her forehead and shirt. The look was actually adorable, not that now was the time to notice things like this. But Jaxon had seen a different side of her this morning, and he liked it.

Luke held up a bag. "I also brought by a few of your things from the cabin. I thought you could use them."

"That's fantastic," Abby said. "Thanks so much."

Jaxon turned back to Luke, sensing there was a deeper reason for this visit. "Did something else happen?"

Something about his brother's demeanor indicated there was more to the story here. Ordinarily, Luke would just send one of his deputies to document the evidence here.

So why had Luke himself come?

Luke shifted. "There is a new update that I wanted to let you know about."

Based on his brother's stiff tone and actions, he was in professional mode. This had something to do with Abby. Jaxon felt certain of it.

He braced himself for whatever he was about to find out.

"What's going on?" Abby rubbed her arms, her apprehension evident.

"I just wanted to let you know that I've been trying to get in contact with your friend Renee to confirm your alibi for the day of the murder," Luke started.

Jaxon felt himself tense as he waited to see where this was going.

"Okay . . ." Abby rubbed her arms more vigorously.

"We haven't been able to get in touch with her, but I made some more phone calls this morning. I discovered she was a victim of a home invasion."

Abby gasped beside him, and her hand flew over her mouth. "What?"

Luke offered a tight nod. "It happened the day after you left to come here to Fog Lake."

"Is she okay?" The question spilled from Abby, and then she seemed to hold her breath.

"She's in the hospital now and sedated. The bullet just missed her lung."

"And her husband? Steve?"

Luke grimaced before quietly saying, "He . . . he didn't make it."

A sob escaped from Abby. She doubled over, and her hands covered her face as obvious grief and shock consumed her. "I can't believe it. Not Steve. Not Renee. Renee..."

Jaxon slipped an arm around Abby, fearing that she might pass out. How much more could she take? The hits just kept coming.

Luke leveled his gaze, sorrow written in the depths of his eyes. "But there's more."

More? Jaxon couldn't even imagine.

He prayed for strength as he braced himself to hear what else his brother had to say. But mostly, he prayed for strength for Abby.

CHAPTER TWENTY-SIX

"MORE?" Abby gasped, her thoughts still swirling. Thank goodness, Jaxon stood next to her, holding her up. Her legs felt like gelatin right now. "How could there possibly be more to the story?"

"The man who did this hasn't been found," Luke said. "He's still at large."

"That's terrible," Abby whispered.

"Was anything stolen?" Jaxon asked.

"Some jewelry."

She squeezed the skin between her eyes. "Steve's life was so much more valuable than some jewelry. How could someone be this ruthless . . . ?"

The way Luke stared at her made her straighten. There was more to this, wasn't there?

Her thoughts raced.

What if the Executioner was behind this? What if that's how he figured out where Abby was?

She lowered herself onto the couch as her head began to swirl.

"What is it, Abby?" Jaxon sat down beside her, his hand going to her back again.

"The cabin where I was staying belonged to Renee's cousin. The car is one of her co-worker's—I paid him cash to use it. What if . . ."

"You think the Executioner is behind this?" Luke asked.

She dragged her gaze up to his. "I don't know."

She wanted to ask if he really thought this man would take it that far. But she already knew that answer. This man was dangerous, and he was unhinged.

"I need to go see her . . ."

"That's not a good idea," Luke said. "I can keep you updated on how she's doing. The detective is going to keep me in the loop since I need to talk to her."

"I guess since Renee can't verify my alibi that I'm still a suspect?" Her voice cracked as she said the words.

Luke's jaw flexed, and he shook his head. "I actually checked your financials. I saw that you used your debit card in Georgia on the day you were supposed to be in Minnesota. I feel fairly confident that you are telling the truth."

Fairly confident? Abby supposed she had to admire his tenacity. She just didn't want to be on this side of the investigation.

"Keep your eyes open. We're keeping our eyes open also. Okay?" Luke locked his gaze with hers.

"I will." She nodded. At least, Abby thought she did.

As soon as Luke stepped out the door and the lock was latched, she felt like she would collapse. Before she could, Jaxon's arms went around her, and he pulled her into a hug.

"It's going to be okay," he murmured.

Abby wished she felt that certain. But she didn't argue. Instead, she let herself fold into his embrace. It was nice not to feel alone in all this. But Jaxon probably had no real clue what he'd gotten himself into right now.

JAXON AND ABBY climbed out of the sedan Luke had let them borrow while Jaxon's truck was being repaired. It was time for Harper's party, which was being held at Boone's place.

Jaxon felt the rush of nerves rake through Abby as they walked up the steps to the front door. "They're going to like you."

"I'm not so sure about that," Abby said. "If I was in their shoes, I would be very skeptical about me being here too."

They paused on the steps, and Jaxon turned toward her. "It might take them some time to warm up, but I'm glad that you're here."

She offered a grateful smile, the moonlight hitting her face and making her look warm and friendly. She'd donned an old scarf and hat to stay warm in the frigid temperatures. The overall picture she formed was adorable . . . and enticing.

"Thank you," Abby finally said, though her eyes still held some doubt.

"Besides, you'll be in good hands here tonight," Jaxon continued. "The sheriff will be here, the fire chief, and a former Army ranger."

His words didn't seem to comfort her. A frown still tugged on her lips. "I only hope I didn't bring trouble with me."

"Someone would have to be pretty brazen to show up here."

She didn't have to say the words for Jaxon to know what she was thinking: The Executioner was pretty brazen. Jaxon pushed down his own nerves.

Abby held her plate of cookies closer as Jaxon knocked on the door to his old family home, the place he'd grown up. Boone and Brynlee lived here now.

A moment later, Luke answered. He already appeared more laid-back in his casual clothing—a long-sleeved T-shirt and jeans. He smiled at Jaxon before extending that same smile to Abby.

"Welcome." He stepped aside and swept his arm out to lead them inside.

Jaxon placed his hand on Abby's back as he directed her into the house. He felt the slight tremor running through her.

He understood it. Which made no sense. Except there was something about Abby that captured all his attention. Maybe in ways that it shouldn't. Romance was the last thing he was looking for. Yet, he couldn't deny there was something about Abby he was drawn to.

"Listen, before you join in the fun, I wanted to let you know that we arrested someone." Luke paused in the foyer and lowered his voice as chatter sounded in the distance.

Abby gasped. "Who?"

Luke pulled up a picture on his phone. "You recognize this man?"

"He's the one from the diner . . . the man who was staring at me."

"A friend of Marissa Wilcox's—she's the woman who disappeared—one of them IDed him as the man Marissa was last seen with. Name is Will Able. It turns out this guy is an attorney. I thought that career was kind of fitting, considering the fact this man calls himself the Judge, Jury, and Executioner."

"I agree," Abby said. "Are you sure it's him?"

"Sure? Not yet. But we're holding him. Turns out he was arrested once for stalking someone."

"That's . . . good news for us, right?" Jaxon said. "If the bad guy is behind bars, we can all take it easy."

"This isn't necessarily the same guy," Luke said.

"What?" Jaxon asked. "You think we have two killers on the loose here?"

"I'm just saying we found another pattern of murders that fit these."

Abby's grip clenched Jaxon's arm. "Where?"

"Minnesota. Four women have died over the past fifteen years. They were all people who'd done something wrong. Two cheated on their spouses.

One was a prostitute. One accused her husband of being abusive."

"You think this guy is the Executioner?" Abby asked.

Luke grimaced. "I'm thinking it's a good possibility."

CHAPTER TWENTY-SEVEN

THE PARTY WAS in full swing by the time Jaxon and Abby joined the crowd.

Jaxon introduced Abby to his sister, Ansley, and Ansley's boyfriend, Ryan. She had already met Harper, the guest of honor. She'd also met Boone. Boone's wife, Brynlee, greeted them too.

The scent of steak floated in the air, making Jaxon's stomach rumble. His family had always liked to cook and eat together.

It was good for them all to be together. Jaxon had missed family times like this. When he was younger, he'd craved going back in time, back to when his mom and dad were both still around.

Before his dad had cancer.

Before his mom left.

Those days had seemed so perfect. Jaxon knew that beneath the surface things were rarely perfect. But those childhood days had seemed idyllic.

As he and Abby stood in the kitchen, Brynlee stopped by with a cookie in hand—one of Abby's cookies.

"You made these?" Brynlee held up a half-eaten treat.

"I did," Abby said.

"Well, they are beautiful."

"Thank you."

"They're tasty too. I heard the Coffee Cafe in town was for sale." Brynlee gave Jaxon and Abby a pointed look. "Maybe you guys could get dibs on it and start your own business."

Funny that she said that since Jaxon and Abby had just been joking about that earlier. But Jaxon hadn't really considered opening a coffee house. He'd only played with the idea of starting a coffee business.

The idea of working with Abby was strangely intriguing, however.

The next two hours seemed to fly by. Though Jaxon could tell Abby was nervous, she loosened up as the night went on. She even smiled and laughed.

Could Abby ever fit in with his family?

The circumstances right now made it hard to gauge the answer to that question. But he'd surprisingly found himself intrigued by their time together—that was, when danger wasn't following their every move.

If Jaxon was smart, he'd put those questions out of his head.

But as he picked up one of the cookies that Abby made, he realized he could see Abby in his life for a long time.

THE PARTY HADN'T BEEN as painful as Abby had feared it might be. Jaxon's family was surprisingly nice, although they were notably guarded. She couldn't blame them given everything that had happened.

As Jaxon went downstairs to play pool with his brothers, Ansley wandered up next to Abby.

Of all the people here, Ansley made Abby the most nervous. The woman was edgy, confident, and obviously protective of her brothers.

"I'm glad you could come." Ansley paused near the dessert table but didn't pick up anything.

"Thank you for having me," Abby said, trying to squelch her nerves.

Ansley leveled her gaze with Abby. "I can see the way Jaxon looks at you. He likes you."

Warmth spread through Abby at the words. Certainly, she hadn't heard correctly. Jaxon was simply a good guy who was trying to do the right thing. He'd be silly to like someone in her situation right now.

"I really appreciate everything he's done for me since I arrived here in town," Abby finally said.

"Don't hurt him."

The breath left Abby's lungs at the stark words. Ansley hadn't come over to be chatty. She'd wanted to make a point.

Abby raised her chin. "Don't believe everything you've heard about me."

"Look." Ansley raised her hands. "I'm not one who's quick to judge. For my whole life, people have judged me. Sometimes I deserved it, and sometimes I didn't. But I didn't come over here to talk down to you or act self-righteous. I like you. I can see that Jaxon likes you. I just don't want to see him get hurt."

"I don't want to see him get hurt either."

Ansley stared at her another moment before

nodding. A moment of understanding passed between the two of them.

"The girls and I are about to start a game of spoons," Ansley said. "Do you want to play?"

Abby released the breath that she held. "I would love to."

Halfway through their game, the doorbell rang. Before Harper could answer, Luke appeared and stepped protectively in front of her. Abby couldn't blame him. With everything that was going on right now, everyone needed to be careful.

Abby's understanding was that the entire family was already here, and she wondered who else might be stopping by.

When Luke opened the door, Abby felt herself go weak.

She blinked, certain that she was seeing things.

But she wasn't.

Patrick Finnegan stood on the stoop.

CHAPTER TWENTY-EIGHT

ABBY FELT herself going into shock. She couldn't move. Couldn't speak.

She could only stare.

At Patrick.

He looked so normal with his broad shoulders, neat brown hair, and engaging eyes.

But he was anything but normal. He was a cheater . . . and maybe a killer.

Jaxon nudged himself in between Abby and the man she'd once thought she loved, and he found the words she was unable to speak. "What are you doing here?"

"Abby, I just want to talk to you," Patrick said over Jaxon's shoulder.

"I don't think that's a good idea." Luke's voice hardened as the relaxed family man persona disappeared. "How did you know to come here?"

Patrick didn't seem to hear him. "Please, Abby. I really need to talk."

Abby took a step back, trembles wracking her body. As she did, Ansley put an arm around her shoulders.

"You need to get out of here," Jaxon said. "What gives you the right just to show up like this?"

"Abby . . ." Patrick continued to peer at her, almost as if he didn't see anyone else. The gleam in his eyes showed that familiar look of desperation. Abby had seen it many times before.

But Abby had never expected Patrick to show up here.

Her thoughts continued to race.

The Wilder family had practically taken her in, and again she had brought danger to their doorstep. The only one who could solve this problem was her. She couldn't let the men do all her dirty work.

She stepped out of Ansley's embrace and toward Patrick. "I'll talk to him."

Everyone in the room seemed to go quiet for a moment before talking all at once.

"That's a terrible idea."

"I don't think you should do that."

"We can get rid of this guy for you."

"No, really. But I want Jaxon and Luke to be with me." Abby could be smart about this.

The two men looked at each other, and then finally they nodded.

"Fine," Luke said. "We're talking on the porch."

Abby pulled her coat over her shoulders before stepping outside with the man. She felt Jaxon's gaze on her. Finally, he reached for her, resting his hand on her lower back. Just that small touch gave her a burst of courage.

Jaxon was nothing like Patrick. Patrick had pretended to be someone he was not. And there was nothing about Jaxon that seemed fake. He seemed to be willing to put himself out there, for the good and the bad.

She was going to need all the courage she could get right now. She pulled her gaze up to meet Patrick's. "What are you doing here?"

JAXON WATCHED THE EXCHANGE. Abby

seemed truly shocked about Patrick showing up, as if she had been taken by complete surprise.

This guy had some nerve just coming here. The thought of it caused a surge of outrage to rush through Jaxon's veins, but he kept the emotion in check. Getting angry would not solve anything right now.

"I had to find you." Patrick's eyes looked red, and white stretched around his pupils. A thin layer of sweat covered his skin. "I need to talk to you."

"I told you." Abby crossed her arms. "I don't want to talk to you anymore. We're done."

"I'm not ready to give up on us." Patrick started to reach for her, but he glanced at Jaxon and dropped his hand. "Can't you see how much I care about you?"

"You were married," Abby said. "I would've never, ever gone on a date with you if I had known that."

"My marriage with Theresa was in trouble. She was talking to her high school ex. We were practically divorced." His hands flew in the air as he tried to drive home the words.

"But you weren't." Abby's voice cracked. "Now I have to live with that every day of my life."

"I'm sorry." Patrick tilted his head, his eyes seeming to implore Abby. "I should've told you."

"You killed Theresa, didn't you?" Abby said, her voice just above a whisper.

Patrick swung his head back and forth, almost too quickly, too erratically. "No, the police are looking for her killer right now. You've got to believe me."

"And what about those emails?" Abby continued. "Did you fabricate those as a means of revenge?"

"I don't know who sent those."

"Do you admit that the two of us never had those conversations?" Her voice trembled as she asked the question.

Jaxon knew how much was on the line with his answer. He held his breath as he waited to see how Patrick would respond.

Patrick glanced at Jaxon and then Luke before finally turning back to Abby. "That's right. We never had those conversations."

Relief flooded through Jaxon. He'd known that was the truth, but it felt good to hear it confirmed.

"How did you find out Abby was here?" Jaxon asked, still trying to put the pieces together.

"Someone called and told me an article came out

saying she'd been spotted in Fog Lake, and I knew this was my chance to talk to her."

Jaxon was surprised that the Minnesota police didn't have him in custody. However, they probably didn't have enough evidence yet.

"And who was this person?" Luke narrowed his gaze as he waited for Patrick's answer.

Patrick shrugged, almost as if he was annoyed. "I don't know. I didn't get his name."

"So a random person just called you and told you that Abby was here in town?" Luke clarified, disbelief tinging his voice.

Patrick added. "That's correct. As soon as I heard that, I knew I had to come find her."

"How did you know she was here right now?" Luke continued, not easing up.

"When I got into town, I went into Hanky's and started asking around. Someone said that there was a party over here and this is where she would most likely be."

Jaxon wanted to be surprised, but, in a small town like this, Patrick could be telling the truth. Everybody knew everyone's business here, especially this time of year when the tourists were mostly gone.

"I'm going to need to take you down to the station and ask you a few questions," Luke said.

Patrick's eyes widened with surprise. "What? I didn't do anything wrong, though. Showing up here at your house isn't a crime."

"No, but we are looking for somebody who has been threatening Abby," Luke said. "And now you end up in town? You just became our number one suspect."

CHAPTER TWENTY-NINE

ABBY PACED BACK and forth once they returned to Jaxon's cabin. She couldn't seem to stop herself as her thoughts raced through everything that had happened.

She couldn't believe that Patrick had shown up in Fog Lake. What in the world had he been thinking? Did he still really hold out hope that the two of them could get back together? He'd lost his mind.

As Jaxon cleaned up some dishes in the kitchen, Abby could feel his gaze on her. He seemed just as disturbed by the fact that Patrick had shown up here as she did.

"Have you heard anything from Luke yet?" Abby stopped pacing long enough to ask the question— even though she knew the answer. She hadn't heard

Jaxon's phone ring, and they'd been together since they left the party.

"No, not yet. I'm sure he'll call if he learns something."

"I just can't get over the fact that Patrick came here," she muttered.

"I think we're all pretty shocked by that."

She leaned against the wall. "Did he really think I was going to run back into his arms?"

"People who are a little crazy can convince themselves of anything."

"I wish I had never met that man. All these problems didn't start until I did." That online dating website had been the worst idea ever.

"At least he admitted that those emails weren't real."

Her gaze latched on to Jaxon's. "Do you believe me now?"

"I wanted to believe you from the start." Jaxon turned the water off and turned to face her. "I just had to be smart."

"I can understand that. I wished I had been smart from the moment I had met Patrick too."

Jaxon dried his hands, left the dishes behind, and crossed the room to meet her. His hands went to Abby's shoulders as he leaned down to meet her eyes. "Everything is going to be okay, Abby."

"What about that missing woman—Marissa Wilcox? Has she been found?"

Jaxon frowned. "Not last that I heard."

"The dogs were supposed to follow her scent."

"They did—and they lost it. If she got into a car, they'd be more likely to lose her scent. It's not a perfect science."

"Maybe she's still alive. I pray she is."

"Me too. We can hope, right?"

Abby forced herself to nod. "Yes, we can."

"Listen, why don't you sit down? Maybe try to relax a little bit until we hear something."

"There's no way I can relax at this point. Even though this Will guy has been arrested, there's another woman missing, there were footprints on your porch last night, and now Patrick is in town."

Jaxon crossed his arms. "Do you think Patrick could be the Executioner?"

Surprise washed through her as she stared at Jaxon. "Do I think Patrick is guilty of murdering these women? I guess I couldn't put it past him since I believe he murdered his wife as well. Do we know when he got into town?"

"I'm sure Luke is checking that out."

"I would think I'd have recognized him when he followed me in the woods, though. I mean, the way he walked or moved or something." She shrugged and shook her head, feeling like the answers should be coming more easily than they were.

"Maybe Patrick is good at what he does and he's good at disguising some of those personality traits."

"Maybe." She shrugged. "I just don't know what to think right now."

Jaxon's phone rang. He put it to his ear and muttered a few things into the mouthpiece. Finally, he ended the call and turned to Abby.

Abby could hardly breathe as she waited to hear what he had to say. "Well?"

"It looks like Patrick's plane ticket was for earlier today. I don't believe he was behind the other things that have been happening here in Fog Lake."

She continued to hold her breath. "Why do I feel like there's a but in there?"

"Luke didn't have enough to hold Patrick on. He hasn't committed any type of crime. Patrick said he was going to go stay at a hotel for tonight. Luke sent one of his deputies over there to check on him, but he was gone. So was his car."

Abby's head began to spin. "So they have no idea where Patrick is?"

Jaxon nodded, his lips pulling down at the edges. "That's correct."

Abby knew. If there was anywhere Patrick was going, it would be here to this cabin to find her.

JAXON DIDN'T like how any of this was playing out. Patrick had the nerve to show up here in Fog Lake. Not only that, but the man had found Abby, going as far as to track her down at Boone's place.

He knew there were no secrets in small towns, but it was a little too easy for bad guys to find them here.

As he continued to clean the kitchen at his cabin, he watched Abby from across the room. It was nearly eleven o'clock, and darkness had long since fallen outside. Abby seemed wide awake, however, as she sat on the couch with a blanket around her, staring at the fire.

She'd really fit in with his family tonight. That thought brought him a surprising amount of delight. More than it should.

If the two of them had met in different circumstances... would they have a chance?

That he even asked the question startled him. He wasn't looking for romance or love.

But was that what he'd found? What he'd stumbled into? It felt like a good possibility.

He'd never met anyone like Abby before. She was strong yet sweet. Colorful but subtle.

Kind of like her sugar cookies.

But she'd be leaving soon—when this mess was all over. And Jaxon still had to figure out what he wanted to do with the rest of his life. This would be the worst time to start a relationship.

It was best if he put these things out of his mind.

He checked his gun again. The bullets were in place.

Then he glanced out his window. If trouble showed up here again tonight, he was going to be ready.

CHAPTER THIRTY

THINGS ARE NOT GOING ACCORDING to my plan, and I was having to come up with an alternate one.

Take last night, for example. I had seen that woman in the car with the other man. Things had been going smoothly after I grabbed her.

Until they had stopped going smoothly.

And now I felt things raveling out of control.

I didn't like it when things raveled out of my control. I prided myself in knowing exactly what I was doing. I could not let this continue.

I sat in my car and stared at the beautiful land-scape around me.

These mountains had served me well since I had been here. But soon, I was going to have to leave.

It was a good thing I had thought of my backup plan. I knew exactly how I could get to Abby—and to Jaxon too.

I tried to whistle, but the sound didn't come as easily as I'd wanted.

I tried again.

Finally, the melody escaped my lips. I never knew what that song was going to be. Today, it was the theme song from *The A-Team*.

A happy little ditty. My dad had taught me that whistling cured everything. The act made people sound confident, made people feel happy. He'd been correct. As long as I still had my whistle, I would be okay.

And I deeply appreciated the old motto from that TV show. *I love it when a plan comes together.*

Yes, I did love it when things worked in my favor.

Tomorrow. It was when everything would need to happen. Everything was in place.

And Abby Brennan had no idea what was coming for her.

The Executioner would do his job.

CHAPTER THIRTY-ONE

WHEN JAXON AWOKE the next morning, he was surprised to see Abby sitting in a chair nearby, his laptop on her legs. She smiled apologetically and closed the screen as she looked at him.

"Hope I didn't wake you," she murmured, looking cozy beneath her blanket and with her hair tousled.

He sat up and raked a hand over his head. "You didn't. I didn't realize I was sleeping so hard."

"You were out and needed some rest."

"I guess I did." He blinked, trying to wake up. "And here I thought you were awake because you were excited about the Hills, Hollows, and Hearts Festival."

That got a small smile out of her, but it quickly

disappeared. She held up his computer. "I actually wanted to look something up. I didn't think you'd mind."

"Of course not. Anything good on there?"

"I know this is going to sound strange, but I'm looking at some pictures of Patrick and Theresa and their families. I keep thinking that whoever is behind this has some connection with them. I just need to figure out what that connection is."

"You don't think the guy from the diner—Will Able—did it?" Jaxon asked.

"I want to believe that. I really do. But my gut tells me he isn't our guy."

Jaxon stood and went to sit on the oversized arm of Abby's chair. "Has anything triggered a memory?"

"Not yet."

Jaxon pointed to the screen, where Patrick stood with three other people. "Do you know who these people are?"

"My understanding is that this woman is Patrick's aunt, this is his dad, and this is his best friend."

"No mom?"

"I'm not sure what happened with her. She died when Patrick was a child, I think."

"I take it you never talked to any of them?"

Abby drew in a breath before letting out a deep sigh. "About a month ago, I got a call from Patrick's dad."

Jaxon turned to her, unable to contain his surprise. It was yet another fact that Abby hadn't shared. But he knew it would be challenging trying to recall everything at once. Certainly, Abby shared things as she remembered.

"Why would his dad call you?"

"It was out of the blue and a little strange. Patrick was the police's number one suspect. I guess that Patrick's dad had begun to suspect that his son might be guilty. He called me to let me know that he was sorry about what his son was putting me through."

"Ouch. To not even have your father believing you must be tough."

"Yes, it is." She sounded like she spoke from experience. "My dad has distanced himself from me since all this happened."

Jaxon squeezed her hand. "I'm sorry to hear about that. We all have our own issues, don't we? We can present the perfect picture on social media, but that's rarely the case when you look deeper."

"You've got that right."

"Did Patrick's dad say anything else?"

"That it was a shame. I wasn't really sure if he

was calling to offer his condolences or to feel me out, to play the good cop and get information from me. Since I never met the man, it's hard to say."

"Were he and Patrick close?" Jaxon asked.

"It was just the two of them while Patrick was growing up. I think Patrick mentioned at one time that his dad had to retire from his job as a veterinarian because of some health conditions."

Jaxon leaned back, trying to think everything through and not miss any angles. "I assume Patrick only called you in private so no one would question him?"

Abby raised one shoulder in a shrug. "For the most part. He had only certain times when he said he could talk. But there were a few times I heard some people in the background. I could tell he was trying to be careful what he said during those times. At the time, I thought he was just being private. But now, looking back, I can see the truth."

As Abby said the words, she stiffened. Her eyes razored back and forth as if she was trying to recall a memory.

"What is it?" Jaxon asked.

"I know I'm going to sound scatterbrained, but I just had a flashback of some sort. I don't know why I haven't thought of this before."

"What is it?" Jaxon leaned closer, anxious to hear what she had to say.

"There was one time when Patrick was talking to me. It was one of those occasions where I could hear things in the background. But there was a song playing."

"What was it?"

"It was 'Little Red Riding Hood.'"

"The same song the Executioner has been whistling when he pursues you?"

Abby's wide eyes met his, and she nodded. "The exact same one."

"So do you think Patrick might be our guy?"

"I have no idea, but maybe it's something we need to explore more deeply."

LUKE SHOWED up thirty minutes later with Jaxon's truck.

"The windshield is fixed," he said.

"Thanks," Jaxon said, grateful for his brother's help.

Luke's gaze went to Abby, and he walked toward her. "I hate to be the bearer of bad news, but the police in Minnesota are coming out to question you today. I wanted to let you know, to give you a heads up."

"Why? How do you know that?" Abby asked.

"They contacted me. They saw the article in the paper about you, and they need to ask some questions about Theresa's death."

Abby swallowed hard. "I understand."

If only she could remain underground for a while longer. But that was just wishful thinking.

"Do the police think she's a suspect?" Jaxon asked.

Luke shrugged. "I can't answer that."

She pressed her hands into her temples. "I don't know how they could think I would be involved with this."

"Someone else has obviously set it up so you can take the fall."

She looked at Jaxon, a million unspoken conversations passing between them. There was so much that she wanted to say. Though she'd only known him and his family for a few days, they already felt like a safety net to her. Maybe she was foolish to think so, but it was the truth.

Luke shifted. "What was Patrick's upbringing like, Abby? I'm trying to get inside his head."

"I was just telling Jaxon this. It was just him and

his dad. My impression is that he was spoiled and got what he wanted."

"I did my own research," Luke said. "Since his mom was found dead with another man, I have to wonder if he grew up in a home where women weren't talked about with respect."

Abby shivered. "I'd say that was a good possibility, especially knowing what I know now. When Patrick and I went scuba diving, our instructor was a woman. Patrick actually asked if we could have a man instead. I questioned him about it, and he seemed to realize what he'd said. He explained that he'd be more comfortable with a male, only because he was anxious about diving for the first time. Maybe I'm stupid, but I bought his explanation. I just thought he was nervous."

"And Theresa's family?" Luke continued. "I know he didn't talk about Theresa, but what's your read on them? I'm sure you've done research."

Abby nodded. "I have. I think her family was the opposite of his. They were large and seemed close-knit. I think Patrick was probably attracted to that. I think he may have felt lonely as a child when his dad was working and without a mom or any siblings."

A better, more complete profile came together in

Jaxon's mind. All the right elements were in place for Patrick to have developed a blatant disregard for women. Maybe he even thought of them as material possessions, ones he could use and abuse as he saw fit.

The thought caused anger to burn inside him.

Before she could say anything, movement outside the window caught her eye, and she froze.

"What is it?" Luke asked.

"I just saw someone outside . . ." she murmured.

"Are you sure?" Jaxon asked.

She nodded. "Positive. He's in the woods."

CHAPTER THIRTY-TWO

JAXON AND LUKE RUSHED OUTSIDE, guns drawn. Jaxon's gaze scanned everything around them.

There.

He saw the movement in the woods, just as Abby had said. He and Luke darted toward the stranger.

This could be the Executioner. This was their opportunity to catch him, to end this once and for all.

Was it Patrick? Or another faceless stranger?

"Police! Put your hands up!" Luke called, his gun drawn and aimed.

Jaxon waited with anticipation of what would happen.

A moment later, a fifty-something man stepped

from behind the trees, his hands in the air. He was big and burly, with dark hair and thick shoulders.

Jaxon blinked, trying to figure out who he was. He looked vaguely familiar, but . . .

"Who are you, and what are you doing here?" Luke demanded.

"I'm here to talk to her." The man shoved his thick finger at Abby.

Luke joined him, putting a barricade between this man and Abby.

"Who are you?" Luke asked.

"That's none of your business," the man said.

"This is Theresa's uncle, Marshall." Abby's voice cut through the tension.

Theresa's uncle was here now?

"Why did you come out here?" Luke asked, his voice still rock hard.

"I came out here because I was following Patrick."

"Why would you follow Patrick out here?" Abby shook her head as if trying to make sense of things.

"Because I'm trying to prove that he's my niece's killer. Name is Marshall Thurman."

"Why don't you come in and have a seat?" Jaxon glanced back at Abby, who nodded in agreement.

A few minutes later, they were all seated at the

table, but the tension remained in the room. This man was big and scary looking. Though Jaxon knew he and Luke could take Marshall, the man still had a threatening disposition, and that made Jaxon uncomfortable.

"Start from the beginning," Luke said.

"I believe that Patrick murdered my niece, and I am going to prove that's what happened if it's the last thing that I do." Marshall's nostrils flared and his eyes narrowed.

"So you followed him here?" Jaxon asked. "Did you hop on the same plane?"

"No, but I've been tracking Patrick's moves. I have someone tailing him, actually. I saw that he came here, and I figured he had a good reason to do so. I also knew that Abby was no longer in Georgia."

Jaxon glanced at Abby and saw her skin go pale.

"Why are you keeping tabs on me?" Abby asked.

"Because I wasn't sure if you were a part of this or not. I no longer believe that you are."

"What changed your mind? That article came out this week with all those fake emails that I supposedly sent to Patrick." Her voice trembled as she said the words.

"I have a feeling that was Patrick's doing. I talked to you before. Those emails didn't even sound like you. Plus, I know that you weren't in Minnesota when she disappeared."

"How do you know that?"

"Because I hired a private investigator to look into you. I know you planned to head to Minnesota, but you changed your mind."

Abby's shoulders seemed to relax. "That's correct."

"My private investigator also discovered that somebody has been threatening you. I don't believe you're guilty. I just want to talk."

"So you're not the one behind those threats toward Abby?" Jaxon asked. He knew that the man wouldn't necessarily be truthful, but he asked the question anyway.

"Me?" Disbelief stretched in his voice. "No. Of course not. I would never do something like that. I only want justice for my niece."

"Who do you think is behind the threats against Abby?" Luke asked.

Marshall shrugged. "Patrick would be my first guess, especially knowing now what he did to Theresa. Anyone who could murder his wife is capable of anything."

Jaxon saw Abby shudder again. He wanted to

reach out to her, to try to comfort her. But this wasn't the time or place.

"When did you get into town?" Luke continued, not softening in the least.

"Last night."

"And how did you know that Abby was here?"

"I saw the article and came to Fog Lake. Once I arrived, I asked around, and people said they'd seen her with Jaxon Wilder. It didn't take that much research to figure out where Jaxon lived."

Jaxon made a mental note that he needed to make it harder for people in the future. Especially considering the enemies he had made.

"What now?" Luke asked.

"What now?" Jaxon echoed, surprise ricocheting through him. "Aren't you going to arrest him?"

"On what grounds?"

"Trespassing." This man had been on his property, if nothing else.

Marshall scowled. "I wasn't trying to trespass. I was only trying to see if Abby was here."

"What do you plan on doing now?" Luke repeated.

"I want to find Patrick."

Luke's steely gaze remained on Marshall. "What will happen when you do?"

The man's nostrils flared. "It will take everything in me not to kill him."

FIFTEEN MINUTES LATER, Luke and Marshall left.

Abby still felt a tremble deep inside her. She couldn't believe Marshall had shown up here. At least, he didn't think Abby was guilty. That had been the one good thing about his unexpected visit.

Jaxon glanced at his watch and frowned.

At once, Abby remembered Jaxon's meeting. "You need to get ready to go."

"I do. But with everything going on . . ."

"I'm not going to be the reason that you lose this deal. I'll go with you."

Jaxon gave her a skeptical glance. "I'm not sure that's a great idea."

"You're meeting him out in public, right?"

Jaxon nodded. "Yes, we're going to meet at the coffeehouse in town."

"What if I go with you but sit at a different table? You'll hardly know that I'm there."

He still seemed hesitant but finally nodded. "If you wouldn't mind doing that, that would be great."

"Of course. Let me just put some lip gloss on and run a brush through my hair, and I'll be ready to go."

A few minutes later, they were in Jaxon's truck.

They headed through town, found a parking space, and a few minutes later stepped into the coffeehouse. It was the first time Abby had been there, and she had to admit that the place had potential.

A whole array of baked goods begged for attention in a display case near the counter. The soothing aroma of coffee filled the room, local artwork graced the walls, and pleasant music played on the overhead.

Was this the shop that Ansley had said was for sale? With a few changes, this place could be a raging success.

But this wasn't the time to think about things like that.

Jaxon's gaze met somebody else's across the room, and he nodded.

Before Abby went her separate way, she squeezed his arm and whispered, "You're going to do great."

"Thanks for your faith in me. Stay close, okay? Promise?"

She nodded. "I will."

Abby found a table two places away. She looked across the room at the man Jaxon was meeting with. He appeared to be in his early thirties . . . and he had a beard.

But that didn't mean he was the man they were looking for. Not every man with a beard was a suspect.

As Abby listened to Jaxon interact with the man, she felt like this was going to be a home run for him. This man would be a fool to pass up Jaxon's coffee.

A surge of delight welled in her. Jaxon deserved all the good things that might come his way. Abby hoped that she wouldn't hold him back.

She looked around, wishing she could celebrate. But that was hard to do with a killer on the loose.

ABBY WAITED until she and Jaxon stepped away from the coffeehouse to say anything. But, as soon as they went outside, the sound of the band playing at the festival overpowered everything else.

Raising her voice, Abby asked, "How did it go?"

"I got an order for one hundred pounds of coffee to start with. They'll serve some and sell it by the package also. If that goes well, he'll add it to all his shops—and he has ten."

Abby squealed and threw her arms around Jaxon. "That's great."

He leaned into her and pulled her closer. "Thank you."

Abby realized what she'd done and stepped

back. What had she been thinking? She needed to keep her distance.

She straightened her shirt and hesitantly pulled her gaze to meet his. "I'm really happy for you, Jaxon."

They started walking back toward his truck. As they did, Abby caught a glimpse of the festival in the town square area. People lingered and danced as Dirk Watson and his band played a slow ballad. String lights were strung overhead, and hearts had been mounted on the light poles.

Abby paused and sighed. It was quite the sight, almost like one of those heartwarming movies come to life.

Jaxon took her hand. "Let's check it out for a minute."

"Really?"

He smiled. "Really."

They cut through the town and stopped on the edge of the festival. It looked like the perfect way to spend the day. Abby spotted the rest of Jaxon's family standing together not far away.

"Can I have this dance?" Jaxon asked.

Abby drew her gaze away from his family and blinked in surprise. "With me?"

A grin tugged at his lips, and he looked around.

"I don't see anyone else nearby that I want to dance with."

Abby thought about it a minute. She wanted to. She really did. But . . . "Do you think that's a good idea with everything that's happened?"

"I always think a dance is a good idea."

Finally, she nodded. "Okay then."

Jaxon took her hand and led her into the crowds. His arms went to her waist, and he pulled her close. Immediately, warmth rushed through her.

She liked the feel of Jaxon beside her. Liked his leathery scent. Liked the muscles beneath her hands.

In fact, she liked Jaxon a little more than she should. If she were honest with herself, she'd admit that he'd consumed her thoughts ever since they'd met.

He leaned closer, his warm breath hitting her cheek. "I promise, I won't let anything happen to you."

Something about his words brought a burst of pleasure through her. He sounded sincere, and, from what she knew of him so far, he was the type of guy who lived out what he believed in. She'd be a fool to ever let someone like him get away.

As the band in the background played, they swayed back and forth to the music.

"You want to hear something crazy?" Jaxon whispered.

"I've had my fair share of crazy lately, but go ahead."

He pulled his head back until their eyes met. "I really like you, Abby Brennan."

Another flash of delight rushed through her. "That is crazy. No one in their right mind should."

He chuckled. "I didn't mean it that way exactly."

"And how did you mean it?"

"I mean that, given the circumstances, there's no way I should be thinking about romance or how beautiful you are or how I feel like we connect in ways that I haven't felt before. Yet, somehow, that's exactly what I'm thinking."

"I can understand that." Her voice nearly cracked as she said the words. Because she meant them.

Jaxon gently stroked his thumb across her cheek. Their gazes met until everything else around them seemed to disappear. Slowly, Jaxon leaned toward her until their lips met.

Warmth exploded inside her, traveling up and down her spine and all the way to her fingertips. Abby never wanted the bliss of this moment to end.

Except…

She stopped swaying and took a step back. A flurry of emotions rushed through her, and she tried to hold back tears. "I can't, Jaxon."

"But I thought you just said you felt the same way."

"I do. And that's my problem. Even though there's nothing I want more than to be lost in this moment with you, I've made some serious mistakes in my past. I dated a married man."

"You didn't know that he was married, though. That's on him."

"Maybe it is, but I still have to live with that for the rest of my life. *That's* a big deal. I have to live with the fact that Patrick murdered his wife so that he could be with me. Maybe I'm not directly guilty, but I *feel* guilty. I feel like I should be punished for that."

"Abby…"

Her eyes met his. "You deserve someone who doesn't come with this kind of baggage, Jaxon."

"Why don't you let me be the judge of that?"

Tears rushed to Abby's eyes, and she quickly wiped them away. She couldn't let herself be happy right now. She didn't *deserve* to be happy. Not after everything that had happened.

Before they could even finish the conversation, someone tapped Jaxon on the shoulder. A man Abby had never seen before stood there. He reminded her slightly of a lumberjack, but the look in his eyes turned her stomach.

What was happening now? Whatever it was, it wasn't good.

"DANNY AXON," Jaxon muttered as he watched the man gloating in front of him. The two of them had never liked each other. Danny was nothing but trouble. Jaxon mostly tried to avoid him, just to keep the drama out of his life. "What do you want?"

Instead of addressing Jaxon, Danny's eyes went to Abby. "I heard who you are."

Jaxon glanced at Abby and saw her go pale. She took a step back.

"You're the other woman. You and your boyfriend killed your boyfriend's wife so you could be together." Danny's loud voice rang out through the crowd until the people dancing around them stopped and stared.

Jaxon saw his family surrounding them, stepping up in case they needed the support.

"Danny, you need to back off," Jaxon said.

"No, everyone here needs to know who this woman really is. She and her boyfriend killed somebody so they could be together."

Gasps sounded around them. Abby buried her face in horror.

"It's not like that," Jaxon said, glancing at the crowd around them.

But they were already taking steps back, judgment already forming.

Jaxon fisted his hands at his side, wanting to give this man a piece of his mind. But Luke touched his arm before he could do anything foolish.

"You don't belong here in this town," Danny told Abby.

"Danny, you're the one who needs to get out of here," Luke growled.

"The perfect Wilder family is coming to the rescue of one of their own." Danny clucked his tongue. "I should've known you all would be here."

"I mean it, Danny," Luke said. "You need to get out of here before I arrest you for disturbing the peace."

Danny narrowed his eyes and took a step back. "While we're sharing secrets, maybe I should tell you all that Jaxon here has been keeping in touch with his mom for the past seven years. Did you guys all know that?"

Ansley turned to Jaxon, her eyes wide and disbelieving. "Is that right?"

"This isn't about me right now," Jaxon said through gritted teeth. "This is about Danny. Don't let him distract you."

"Little Jaxon betrayed all of you," Danny continued, a taunting tone to his voice. "How does that make you all feel?"

As Jaxon glanced back at his siblings, he realized Danny had succeeded in doing exactly what he'd set out to do: the troublemaker had put a wedge between them.

CHAPTER THIRTY-FOUR

ANSLEY STARED AT JAXON, something dark and angry in her gaze. "You've been meeting with Mom?"

"It's not like it sounds," Jaxon said, his chest tightening.

"Then what exactly is it?" Ansley demanded.

Jaxon raised his hands in the air. This wasn't the place that he wanted to get into it, but it appeared he'd been forced into this position.

"I know that none of you want Mom to be a part of your life. And I get it. I know why. But that's not what I wanted for myself. Despite everything that she's done, I still love her. Maybe that makes me a bad person. Maybe it makes me naïve or stupid. I don't know. But I couldn't cut her out of my life."

"She betrayed us," Ansley said. "She left us when we needed her the most."

"I know, and she lives with that guilt every day."

"If she felt so guilty about it, then why didn't she tell us that?" Ansley said. "I've never once heard her say she's sorry."

"Have any of you ever given her the chance to say sorry?" Jaxon asked. "Look, she's not perfect. She's made a lot of mistakes. So have all of us."

"I just can't believe you would keep this from us." Ansley crossed her arms.

"It was because I didn't want a situation like this," Jaxon said. "I wasn't going to push it on any of you. But it's a choice that I made for my life."

"There's nothing wrong with Jaxon being friendly with Mom," Luke said. "It's his choice. Boone invited her to his wedding. I visited her in the hospital."

"That's different. When none of us had anyone else, we had each other," Ansley said. "I didn't know he was standing with the other side."

"There are no sides here," Luke said. "Each of us wages our own battles. Don't we all know that by now?"

No one said anything for a minute.

That was when Jaxon saw movement out of the corner of his eye. It was the same shadowed figure he'd seen twice before. The one who'd been at the hospital and on the sidewalk.

"Keep an eye on Abby," he said. "I'll be right back."

And with that he took off toward the figure in the distance.

ABBY FELT the heat rise to her cheeks as she watched the confrontation between Jaxon and his family. She knew it was a sticky situation, and that there were no easy answers. But it was still so painful to see how mistakes from the past could tear a family apart.

She prayed that this would not be a definitive moment in their relationship, but that they could pull through this and still come together.

What Jaxon's mom had done was wrong, but that didn't mean that reconciliation wasn't possible. Abby didn't want to say whether that was the right or the wrong thing. But she did know that forgiveness was an absolute must.

As the siblings talked quietly amongst themselves, Abby realized that she shouldn't be here. They needed to have their own moment to process this.

And where had Jaxon gone? What or who had he seen? Was it the Executioner?

She shivered and rubbed her arms as she glanced around the crowd. No one else seemed to have noticed what had happened. People had gone back to dancing, the band still played, and everything looked idyllic.

Abby leaned back against one of the buildings, trying to stay out of everyone's way while still remaining close. Occasionally, she saw Luke glancing over at her to make sure that she was okay.

But when someone tapped on her shoulder, she turned to see someone that she didn't expect. A woman.

"Abby Brennan?"

Abby tensed. "That's me."

"I'm Detective Cait Kovach with the Minneapolis Police Department. I need to ask you a few questions." She held up a badge.

Abby glanced at it and saw it looked legit.

She glanced at Luke and Boone and saw they were deep into a family discussion.

"Luke!" she called, pointing to the detective.

Luke glanced over, saw the detective, and nodded. "I'll be right behind you."

CHAPTER THIRTY-FIVE

JAXON CUT THROUGH THE CROWDS, determined not to let this guy get away again. But the sheer amount of people out in town was going to make this harder.

Or maybe he could use it to his advantage.

He veered to the right, staying close to the sidewalk, and paused. In the distance, he saw the man in black still jogging away. He was headed toward the parking lot at the edge of town, Jaxon realized.

Jaxon took a shortcut through an alley between two buildings, took a couple more turns, and stopped just before the lot.

He spotted the man.

He was younger than Jaxon had assumed, and his black clothing appeared to be jeans and a dark shirt with a leather jacket. The man glanced behind him and slowed his steps, as if he assumed he'd lost Jaxon.

He was in for a sad surprise.

Before the man could see him, Jaxon ducked behind a car one vehicle over from the black Volvo he'd spotted earlier. As soon as he heard the man's footsteps, he leapt from his hiding spot, grabbed the man, and jerked his arms behind him.

The man groaned.

"Who are you, and why are you following me?" Jaxon demanded.

When Jaxon had initially began chasing the man, he was sure that had something to do with Abby. Was this the Executioner?

The man seemed too young. But it could be a reporter. Maybe even the reporter who had spilled the beans about where Abby was staying.

"It's not what you think," the man said through gritted teeth.

"Then you better start explaining."

"I will, I will. But you need to let go of me first."

"That's not going to be happening. You've been eluding me for the past three days."

"I promise I can explain. Reach in my back pocket and pull out my wallet."

Still holding the man's arms behind his back, Jaxon released one of his hands and grabbed the man's wallet.

What was inside surprised even him.

ANOTHER SURGE of anxiety went through Abby as she followed the detective through the crowds. This woman just needed a moment of her time, and then Abby could return to the Wilder family.

The detective in front of her remained cold and professional. Abby couldn't get a good read on her, except that she'd come a long way to talk to Abby.

The only comfort Abby found was in knowing that the Executioner was most definitely a man. This woman could not be the person pursuing her. The fact made her feel a little better.

The woman reached a dark sedan with rental plates on the back and opened the door. "This will be the best place for us to talk," she said. "It will be private, and Sheriff Wilder can meet us here."

Abby took one last glance back to the celebration in Fog Lake. Crowds still danced to the music. The band was loud, and she could hear the lyrics, "Our

last Valentine's Day. I never thought you'd go away . .
."

How appropriate.

Finally, she slipped inside the sedan. Nausea again roiled in her stomach. She might as well get this over with.

Just as the detective started to slip inside, a strange sound filled the air. The roar of the music made it hard to distinguish, but it almost sounded like . . .

The detective slipped to the ground.

Abby lurched. A blot of blood formed on the woman's white shirt.

A gunshot. It had almost sounded like a gunshot.

Abby reached for the door handle beside her and jerked it. But it was locked. The only way she could get out was to go over the detective.

Before Abby could, a man grabbed the keys from Cait's hand, climbed into the driver's seat, and slammed the door.

A man wearing a blue hat and a jacket.

It was the Executioner. He'd finally found Abby, and now it was too late to escape.

CHAPTER THIRTY-SIX

"YOU'RE TELLING me you're who?" Jaxon still couldn't believe what he was hearing.

"My name is Ted Lamariski, and I'm with the CIA."

"Why have you been following me?" Jaxon released the man after seeing his official ID, but he still remained on guard. He couldn't trust anyone right now.

Ted straightened his jacket and took a step back, raising his hands in the air. "Sorry, man. I wasn't trying to scare you."

"I didn't say you scared me, but you definitely had me curious. You've been following me."

"I was sent here to recruit you for the CIA."

"The CIA? Why would I want to join the CIA?" His words made no sense.

"We heard about the work that you did over in Iraq, and we knew that you had decided not to reenlist. We thought you would be a perfect fit for us."

"So you followed me?"

"My boss sent me here to check you out first. He wanted to make sure you were the person he thought you were before we made you an offer. I've been in the information collecting phase."

"So you're a spook?" This whole thing seemed surreal—and irritating.

"Not exactly. I'm just a recruiter. As you know, the CIA does not work on US soil. But we do recruit here."

"I don't know why you would think I would be a good fit for you."

"You have a reputation as someone who has integrity, who likes to fight for what is right, but who ultimately listens to orders."

Nailah's face fluttered through Jaxon's mind. Were they commending him for letting an innocent woman die? Anger burned inside him. That wasn't the person he wanted to be.

"I'm not the guy you want," Jaxon said.

He started to take a step away, when Ted grabbed his arm. "I just need you to think about it."

Jaxon bristled. "I've already thought about it. I'm not interested."

"We know what happened with Khalshazar's wife."

Jaxon froze and stared at him. "And?"

"We knew that you were going to help her, and we know that her husband killed her before you could."

His heart pounded in his ears. "And that's the kind of person you're looking for?"

"We're looking for people who have a good instinct and who want the best for our country."

"So letting her die was the best thing for our country?" The words left a bitter taste in his mouth.

"I didn't say that. In fact, we were hoping to make her an asset instead of her husband."

Realization spread through Jaxon. "Then why didn't you guys tell me to help?"

"We were on the verge of doing so when she died. We never suspected that was going to happen as it did. In fact, one of our guys talked to her, and that's what set her husband off."

"I thought it was because she talked to me." His heart beat harder.

"As far as we know, Khalshazar didn't know anything about that."

Stunned, Jaxon stepped back. All the guilt that he'd been feeling had been for nothing. Well, maybe not nothing. Nailah had still died, and he still felt pangs of grief about that. But it wasn't his fault . . .

Ted extended his arm and shoved something into Jaxon's hand. Jaxon saw it was a business card.

"Think about it, and give me a call," Ted muttered.

Before Jaxon could respond, Ted got into his car and took off.

Jaxon had to get back to Abby now. He was so ready to have all this behind them.

At least one mystery had been solved.

ABBY FELT herself beginning to hurl, but the action never materialized. She pressed herself into the far corner of the car, as far away from this man as she could get. Not that it would help. She was trapped.

She tugged on the door handle again. Pounded on the tinted window. No one could see her. No one could hear her screaming over the music.

As the Executioner pulled away from the scene, Abby's gaze darted. Where was Luke? Jaxon?

Just then, Luke and Boone appeared from the alley. They glanced around, as if looking for her.

But it was too late. They couldn't see her inside the car. Instead, they spotted the detective on the ground and sprinted toward her.

The Executioner was going to get away with this. Abby felt certain of it.

A low moan escaped from her. This was how it was all going to end.

"I never thought I'd get a moment alone with you," the man said.

Trembles claimed Abby's entire body at the sound of his voice. She tried to get a good look at him, but all she could see was the side of his face. His hat still shadowed much of his features, his beard masked his face, and his jacket concealed his body.

Was it Patrick?

She'd think she would know something like that at this point. But it was hard to see.

"Why are you doing this?" Abby could hardly understand her own voice because of the way it quivered.

"Don't you know that by now?"

The calmness of his words caused another deep shiver to claim her. She wrapped her arms over her chest. "I didn't kill Theresa."

"I didn't say you did."

What? Wasn't that what all of this was about? "Then why are you doing this? Why are you punishing me?"

"Because all this is your fault." His voice took on the singsongy tone again. "All of this was started because you put the idea in someone's head."

"What idea?" Abby had no clue what he was talking about.

"The idea that Patrick could have a better life with you."

"I didn't know he was married." Tears rushed down Abby's cheeks again. It didn't seem to matter how much time had passed, guilt still flooded Abby every time she thought about it. "I would've never met up with him if I had known."

"That's what they all say."

What they all say? What did that even mean?

She didn't have time to figure it out now.

Abby had to figure out a way out of this car. But how? They were getting farther and farther away from the downtown area. What was his plan for her?

Just as they pulled onto the highway leading

along the side of the lake, the man raised his hand. He held something. The next instant, spray filled the vehicle.

Abby coughed, desperate to get the substance out of her lungs. What was that?

Before she could dwell on it, she felt herself getting woozy.

It must have been some kind of spray that would make her pass out, she realized. Panic tried to claim her.

Abby tried to fight it, but it was no use. Her eyelids became heavier and heavier.

The next thing she knew, everything went black.

CHAPTER THIRTY-SEVEN

JAXON GLANCED AROUND as he reached his family. He wasn't looking forward to the aftermath of their conversation, and he knew they were probably still angry. Especially Ansley.

They were never supposed to find out like that. But another part of him felt good knowing that it was all out in the open now. There were no more secrets. His family could choose whether to accept or to reject him because of his decisions. But he didn't regret his relationship with his mom.

He had other matters to attend to before diving into his family drama again. He spotted Luke bent down near someone on the ground. It was a woman. Blood blotted her shirt.

"It's the detective from Minnesota," Luke told

him, pressing a cloth on her chest. "Cait Kovach. I met her an hour or so ago. Paramedics are on the way."

"Where's Abby?"

"She was with the detective," Luke frowned. "I don't know where she is now, Jaxon. I'm sorry."

Concern ricocheted through Jaxon. "You mean you lost her?"

Luke motioned to one of his deputies. "Come hold this on her chest."

As the deputy took over for him, Luke turned to him. "I'm going to put an APB out for her now. We're going to find her."

Jaxon glanced around. "No one saw anything?"

"No."

Jaxon knew what had happened. The Executioner had grabbed her. And there was no telling where he might be with her now.

He felt like he'd been punched in the gut. He had to find Abby. Her life was on the line. He had no doubt about that.

Luke's radio crackled. "Sheriff, we've got someone at the hospital you're going to want to see."

"I'm in the middle of something right now."

"It's the woman who was missing," the

dispatcher said. "You'll want to hear what she has to say."

~

ABBY AWOKE TO DARKNESS. Cold, cold darkness.

At once, everything flashed back to her, and she tried to jump to her feet.

She couldn't.

Her arms were tied behind her. Her legs bound to a chair.

Despite the feel of the rope around her, she tugged her limbs, trying desperately to move, to not feel like an insect trapped in a spider's web.

But she couldn't.

Her breaths came faster now, more shallow.

The Executioner had tied her up somewhere. She was still upright. The ropes must be attached to a wall of some sort.

What was this man planning to do with her? Where was the man now? Was he sitting in the dark, watching her, waiting for her to wake up?

Abby had no idea. But she needed to think quickly.

She glanced around, praying for her vision to clear. For the darkness to somehow fade.

As she blinked several times, her eyes adjusted. She was in some kind of small living room area. A compact couch was against the wall across from her. There were no windows in this room, but light spread from a doorway at the top of a small set of stairs.

Something about the room was strange . . . the height of the ceiling. The whole feel of the place, for that matter. Plus, there was a strange scent.

Just where had this man taken her?

As she felt herself jostle, she froze. Jostle? Why in the world was she swaying back-and-forth?

Before she could think about it much longer, the door opened, and she heard heavy footsteps coming down to meet her.

A half-moan, half-scream escaped her lips as she anticipated the pain to come.

CHAPTER THIRTY-EIGHT

JAXON WENT with Luke down to the hospital. Whoever this Executioner was, he was smart enough not to keep Abby in the downtown area. He was happy that Boone and Ryan were there to keep searching, just in case. But this guy had taken her somewhere. Jaxon had no doubt in his mind about that.

A woman lay in the hospital bed, bandages on her head, her blonde hair a mess around her face.

Luke paused beside her and introduced himself. "Can you tell us what happened?"

"I did something I shouldn't have." She sniffled and glanced out the window as if holding back a sob. "My husband and I have been having problems, so when I met Ralph while I was here, I decided just to forget my problems and have a little fling. It wasn't even a real fling, but we did kiss. Then I got cold feet and realized that I couldn't cheat on my husband like this. Ralph dropped me off at my car, but, as I was standing outside, I heard somebody. It was a man. He said he had lost his dog."

Jaxon felt the air leave his lungs.

"I told him I hadn't seen any dogs. As I turned to leave, he said I had to pay the price for my sins. He sprayed something in my face. I don't even know what it was, but everything went black. When I woke up, I was in the trunk of a car. I heard him outside. He was whistling, but the sound faded. I saw that as my opportunity to do something. I found an emergency latch and got out."

"What happened next?" Luke asked.

"I started running. I was in the woods, maybe at an old campground. I had a feeling he was living there. It didn't matter. I just ran. The next thing I knew, I was lost. I had no idea where I was. Every direction looked the same. But I didn't see the man. That was all I cared about."

"And then?" Luke continued to pry.

"I didn't think I was going to make it, but I just kept running for as long as I could. But the more I ran, the more lost I became. I didn't think I was going to get out of the woods alive." She shuddered and glanced out the widow, drawing in a shaky breath.

"How did you end up here?" Jaxon asked.

"I managed to find a road. I kept walking along the edge of it, and I eventually reached the town."

"Is there anything you can tell us about the man who abducted you?" Luke asked.

"No, I really couldn't tell much about him." She drew in another shaky breath and squeezed her eyes shut.

A nurse bustled in and began checking her vitals. Maybe the lull in the conversation would be good, would give her time to collect herself.

As soon as the nurse left, Luke quietly asked, "Could you identify him if you had to?"

Marissa shrugged. "I don't know. Maybe."

"If we showed you some pictures, could you tell us if any of the faces look familiar?" Luke asked.

"I suppose." She shrugged. "I could try at least."

Luke pulled out his phone and hit the screen. He then handed the device to Marissa, and she began to scroll through.

She stopped on one photo. "This man. He looked like this man. Except, there was something different about him."

Luke took the phone from her, and he and Jaxon looked at it.

Patrick Finnegan's picture stared back at them.

Had Patrick been behind this the whole time? How was that even possible if he had just flown into town the day before?

"I need to put an APB out for him and call for some backup," Luke muttered.

He didn't need to say any more. Jaxon knew they had a deranged killer running loose here in Fog Lake.

Now this man had Abby in his grip. Anger—and worry—flared inside him at the thought.

ABBY TRIED TO BREATHE, but air only entered her lungs in short, pathetic spurts. As much as she tried to control her panic, it didn't matter. Nothing worked.

The man slowly thudded down the stairs, remaining silent. The shadows concealed him, masking his features.

But the fear he caused was all too real.

There was something familiar about him, but

Abby didn't know what. His voice was . . . she'd heard it before somewhere. But it almost sounded like he tried to disguise it now. Just like he was still trying to conceal his identity by wearing that hat, that beard, that jacket.

"I've been waiting for this day for a long time." He paused in front of her.

"I don't know why you want to punish me. I'm telling you, I didn't do any of this on purpose."

"Sin doesn't have to be purposeful."

Abby wasn't sure about the truth in that statement. She only knew that this man was convinced his words were the truth. There was no way that she was going to change his mind. Her only hope was that she might be able to escape.

She tugged her arms and her legs again, but it was no use. The ropes around her were too tight, too thick, too strong.

"If you let me go, I won't tell anybody." Abby's words were desperate. She wasn't even sure if she meant them. But she was willing to try anything right now to get away, to avoid the torture that she knew was coming.

There was nothing to stop him from carrying through with his threats. He would break each of her bones until she went as limp as a rag doll.

"I'm trying to figure out where I want to start," the man said.

"By letting me go?"

He chuckled. "I have to admit, you're persistent. That's probably how you get away with things so often."

"I'm telling you, I don't try to get away with anything." Fear clawed into her voice.

"Most sinners don't realize what they're doing. It's like boiling a crab. It happens so gradually that you don't realize that eventually you're going to be cooked."

"I still don't know why you're targeting me. Plenty of people sin. In fact, we all do."

"Somebody has got to be the example for all those other women out there."

"Why me? Why not Patrick? Why don't you hold him responsible?" It wasn't that Abby wanted this man to go after Patrick, just that she needed to buy herself time. Maybe if she did, Jaxon would find her.

Please, Lord . . .

Her breath caught at the thought of Jaxon. How could she have come to care about him so quickly, so deeply?

When she thought about their kiss, everything in the world felt right. It was just for a moment, but a moment was enough. But she meant what she said when she told him that she didn't deserve him.

If she got out of this situation alive, Abby wanted to have a long talk with him. She wanted to work out all the issues that plagued her. If she did, maybe she would have a chance for happiness again.

Maybe.

The man reached behind her and touched her finger.

Abby sucked in a deep breath.

She waited. Anticipated the pain. Waited for him to fulfill his threat to break every one of her bones.

Her heart pounded in her chest.

Thump. Thump. Thump.

The man gripped her fingertip. Tugged it. Toyed with her.

A cry escaped from her lips.

He seemed to like the sound. Even in the dark, she saw him smile.

This man was sick. Really sick.

"Now, let the fun begin," he muttered.

CHAPTER THIRTY-NINE

JAXON GRABBED his phone and typed in a few things. A moment later, he showed the screen to Marissa. "Is this what the man looked like?"

She took the phone from him and shrugged. "Maybe. It was hard to see his face, like I said. But there are some similarities."

"Who is it?" Luke asked.

"This is Patrick's father. Abby showed me a picture of him on the computer this morning. Said he seemed like a nice guy. He even called at one point about a month ago to express his condolences over everything that had happened because of his son."

Luke clucked his tongue. "I'm not sure what sense this is all making."

"I'm not sure how I could've seen this guy face-to-face and not put it together." Jaxon's jaw tightened as he remembered the encounter he'd had with the man at his house when Abby had first arrived—the man who'd been looking for his dog.

The Executioner had walked right up to his doorstep, and Jaxon had been clueless.

"Don't beat yourself up over it," Luke said.

"He was right there, Luke. I didn't even see it. He even had that mustache and beard. I didn't recognize him."

"The important thing is that we find this guy now. In order to do that, we may need to find Patrick so we can figure out how he thinks."

"That's going to be a challenge since we've been looking for him for the past twenty-four hours with no luck."

"Maybe our luck is about to change." Luke glanced at his phone. "It looks like someone sighted Patrick."

AS THE LIGHT from the stairway hit the man's face, Abby gasped. "Mr. Finnegan?"

She blinked, certain that she was seeing things.

This could not be Patrick's father. Why would he be the one who was behind this?

"You didn't suspect it was me, huh?" he chuckled.

"Why would I? You were nothing but kind to me when you called."

"I was trying to feel you out. I could tell you felt no remorse. That's when I knew I had to do something."

"You don't know me. You don't know how I've been feeling. About how much sleep I've lost as I've been thinking this through. You have to believe me."

"My days of believing people are done. My first mistake was when I married my first wife, Hazel.

Abby pulled in another trembling breath. She was just delaying the inevitable, yet the questions burned in her head. "What happened with Hazel?"

"She cheated on me. I caught her. I made sure the two of them paid."

Abby felt more air leave her lungs. "You killed her?"

"It was a simple house fire that they both happened to get caught in. No one even suspected that I had done it. It was better that way. I couldn't raise Patrick with a mom who would betray us like that."

"Couldn't you have just gone through counseling

or something? Don't get me wrong, it was a terrible thing she did to you. But setting the house on fire?"

"Hazel threatened my manhood with her actions. She was poised to ruin my reputation. Somebody else could have taken over the life that I'd worked so hard to build. I couldn't let that happen, especially since I sacrificed everything for my wife. Look at the thanks I got."

Even though it was hard to see, Abby sensed his growing agitation. His actions seemed quicker, tighter. His breaths were shallow and fast.

"What do you mean by sacrificing everything?" she asked.

"I was set to go to college, but then she convinced me to marry her."

"Convinced you?"

"She said she was pregnant."

"Do you think she said that just to get you to marry her?" Abby tried to put the pieces together.

"I know she did. She was never pregnant. She just wanted to get away from her family, and I was an easy way to do that. I knew within six months of marrying her that I'd made a terrible mistake."

"I still don't understand why this means you're coming after me."

"Because women like you need to be stopped."

"But I tried to end things with your son. Why aren't you trying to punish him?"

"Because men are powerless in front of women. He was your puppet."

"That's not true. He was the one calling most of the shots. At least, he was until the day I broke up with him."

The man's hand flew across her face. "Silence! Enough talking. Now I need to carry through on my promise to break your bones one by one."

Pain throbbed in her cheek, and tears pushed themselves out.

"I'm not Hazel," Abby whispered.

"You don't have to be."

But as the Executioner reached for her hand again, suddenly the whole room shifted. What was going on?

CHAPTER FORTY

JAXON AND LUKE climbed into Luke's SUV and rushed to the area where Patrick had been spotted. As they did, Luke made several phone calls, trying to trace Ron Finnegan's financials and see if they could track him down that way.

As Jaxon thought about it further, those cabins that had been closest to him had been empty. He should've seen this sooner. When that man came down the shoreline looking for his dog and then Jaxon had seen the closest cabins were unoccupied, he should've put the pieces together.

He would have to kick himself later. Right now, he just had to concentrate on finding Abby.

Luke ended the call and turned toward him. "You really care about her, don't you?"

Jaxon stared out the window, trying to make sense of his feelings. "I do. I know it probably seems too fast, but I do."

"Situations like this can accelerate things."

"You sound like you speak from experience."

"I never expected to meet Harper and feel the way I did, either." Luke and Harper had met while tracking down a serial killer also. The last thing Luke had wanted was to fall in love with a journalist —but he had. And he'd fallen hard.

"We've got to find her, Luke." Jaxon's voice waivered as he fought to control his anxiety.

"I know. I'm sorry that I even took my eyes off her for a moment, but—"

"It doesn't matter anymore. We just need to find her."

They pulled up to the scene and saw another sheriff's cruiser. The deputy stood beside someone— Patrick Finnegan. The man was bundled in what almost looked like a snowsuit. His face was red, probably from the cold. A small tent was set up in the distance.

Patrick must have been staying there while he was in town.

Luke and Jaxon rushed over to him, and Luke lit into him. "Where are they?"

"Who are you talking about?" Patrick stared at them as if perplexed.

"Where are Abby and your dad?" Luke demanded.

"My dad? Why would you be asking about my dad?"

"Because your dad grabbed Abby," Luke growled.

Patrick's face paled. "That doesn't make any sense. Why would he do that?"

"You tell us," Jaxon said.

Patrick ran a hand through his hair and shook his head before letting out a long, heavy sigh. "Oh man. How could I not have seen this?"

"Seen what?" Luke said.

"My dad has always carried a chip on his shoulder for women. He's never spoken highly of them, especially not after my mom died in a housefire."

"What happened?"

"It was electrical." Patrick shifted, as if uncomfortable. "There was another man there with her. Not my dad."

Patrick's face went even paler, almost as if he was for the first time exploring the possibility that it hadn't been an accident.

"Did your dad ever say anything to you about Abby?" Jaxon asked.

"Nothing positive. He just grumbled about how he told me so. How I should've never fallen for that woman."

"Where might your dad be now?" Jaxon fisted his hands at his side and used every ounce of his self-control not to be more aggressive than he should.

"I don't know." Patrick's words came out fast, hurried—nearly frantic. "I have no idea. I didn't even know he was here."

"Why are you here at the lake now?" Luke pushed.

"Because I've always loved the water. My dad and I used to rent a houseboat every summer—"

"A houseboat?" Luke asked.

Jaxon and Luke exchanged a glance.

"Yes, that's right. A houseboat." Patrick shrugged, the skin between his eyes knotting in confusion.

Luke grabbed his radio. "We need to find Al. See if he's renting any houseboats right now. Then we need to get a police boat out here to search these waters."

"Wait . . ." Patrick froze. "Do you think my dad rented a houseboat and grabbed Abby?"

Luke said nothing.

"You have to understand one thing," Patrick said. "My dad has trouble seeing because of his cataracts. I really hope he didn't go out on a boat, especially not with the wind and fog like it is now."

Jaxon and Luke glanced at each other again. They had no time to waste.

CHAPTER FORTY-ONE

ABBY FELT the room rocking back and forth. As it did, Mr. Finnegan flew against the wall and muttered something beneath his breath.

"What's going on?" None of this made sense. Where were they, and why was everything moving?

"We must've hit something," Mr. Finnegan muttered.

Hit something?

A boat, she realized.

Suddenly everything made sense. They were in a houseboat of some sort, on one of the lower levels. The windows had been blacked out somehow.

As Abby continued to turn sideways, she realized this wasn't good. The first trickle of water crept in through the ceiling. She pulled with her hands and feet, feeling trapped. Because she *was* trapped. She was helpless to escape.

"You've got to let me loose," she said. "Please."

Mr. Finnegan pushed himself to his feet and shook his head. "No, I can't do that. This wasn't the way I planned it, but it's the way it's going to have to be."

"Please! You can't leave me down here to die."

He staggered toward the stairway, which was no longer upright. "Sometimes things have a way of working out for the best. You won't be hurting anybody else anytime soon."

A deep cry escaped from Abby. She couldn't die like this. As more water rushed in, she pulled at her bonds again. It was no use. They were too tight, and there was no way she could grab anything to let herself loose.

Or was there?

As the boat tilted even more, items began to pummel the area around her. They fell from the tabletop drawers beside the couch that had once been in front of her.

Another jolt, and the couch landed near her feet, barely missing her.

Her breaths came even faster, as she realized she was in even more danger than she had anticipated.

She glanced around, desperate to see the items that had fallen out. One object caught her eye as a sliver of light caused it to glimmer.

Was that a . . . pocketknife?

It appeared to be.

Abby strained to reach it. If she could only grab it and manage to open the blade . . . maybe she could cut through the ropes.

It was the only option she had right now. At least it was something. The possibility was better than no hope at all.

TEN MINUTES LATER, Luke and Jaxon were on a police boat. The weather had turned frigid, especially out here on the water. As the wind swept over the lake, everything around them seemed to frost over. It wouldn't surprise Jaxon if it snowed again a little later.

Not only that, but the waves had also picked up. As the front of the boat collided with the moving water, everyone on board bounced, their bodies jarring uncomfortably. Jaxon didn't care. Not now. All he could think about was finding Abby.

He scanned the lake around them. He knew

there were mountains at the perimeter, along with a few docks jutting out from the shoreline. But the fog had settled again. Nature wasn't going to be their friend right now. In fact, their visibility was almost zero.

"He couldn't have gone but so far away from the shore," Luke shouted over the motor.

"My gut tells me we don't have much time."

"Then we better kick this into high gear. But we're going to need to watch for rocks."

A lot of people didn't know about the rocks that hid beneath the surface of the water, especially closer to the shoreline. It really could be dangerous water to navigate if you didn't know what you were doing.

That thought didn't make Jaxon feel any better.

He pulled out his binoculars and tried to search beyond the fog for a sign of the houseboat. Though the lake was large, finding her wasn't impossible. It would just take time.

Dear Lord, please be with Abby. Keep her safe.

They continued to cruise over the water's surface, bumping with every new wave. Icy precipitation chilled his skin. The temperature was definitely dropping again.

Just what was Mr. Finnegan planning to do with

Abby? Every time the question entered Jaxon's mind, his stomach twisted. He could barely stand to think about it, but the fact that they were out here on the water made things even more dangerous. It added another layer of deadliness.

"Luke!" Jaxon called. "Over there."

He pointed to something in the distance. Was that a houseboat? That's what it looked like to him.

But as they got closer, Jaxon saw that it was tilted on its side . . . sinking.

CHAPTER FORTY-TWO

IT TOOK A FEW TRIES, but Abby managed to open the knife.

Thank You, Jesus.

She'd been nearly certain that it wasn't going to work. Now she held the blade and carefully tried to saw the rope near her wrist. It was harder than she had thought it would be, given the angle of the ropes and her hand. But she was determined not to give up.

Water rushed into the boat. The icy moisture tried to send her body into shock.

Abby continued to run the blade over the rope. Where had Mr. Finnegan gone? Was he somehow escaping? Or was he planning more ways to make her suffer?

Abby couldn't think about that right now. She just needed to think about trying to get out of here.

Finally, one of the ropes broke. A surge of victory rushed through her.

With her hands now free, she began working her other bindings. A few minutes later, another rope broke free.

More water rushed inside, covering her legs. Abby knew she wouldn't survive long in these conditions. It was too cold. Her body would go into shock. Hypothermia would set in.

She reached down and worked the rope around her leg.

As soon as the rope loosened, she sprang toward the stairway. Toward freedom.

Before she could reach the steps, the door slammed shut. Abby raced up the stairs and grabbed the handle. Pounded on the door. Pushed.

It didn't budge.

What happened?

As she pounded again, whistling floated in from the other side. The Executioner had locked her in here.

Abby knew with certainty there was no way out. That door had been her last hope.

~

LUKE IDLED as close as he could to the houseboat. At the first chance, Jaxon hopped on board. He drew his gun. He was going to have to be careful. This vessel wasn't secure, and it could tip at any minute.

Was Abby inside? He hoped the answer was no. He also hoped the answer was yes. Jaxon needed to find her, but he needed for her to be okay.

"Be careful," Luke said behind him.

Another deputy followed behind them, and one stayed on the motorboat. Everything was slippery as the houseboat continued to move, to sink farther under the water.

The shoreline was only ten feet away. They must've hit one of the boulders and turned, he realized.

Where was Ron Finnegan? Was he still lurking close?

"Abby!" Jaxon called.

If she was inside this boat, there was a good chance she was underwater.

Moving quickly, he found the door to the cabin below. Just as he grabbed the handle, a gunshot rang out.

He ducked behind a railing and peered out. Mr.

Finnegan stood behind a tree in the woods, a gun in his hand. The man was shooting at them. The lake was shallow enough here that he must have made a run for it.

"I'll cover you!" Luke said.

Shoving his gun into his waistband, Jaxon grasped the door, trying to get it open.

"Jaxon?" someone called on the other side.

Abby . . . that was Abby. His heart sped.

"I'm here." He pulled harder, more furiously. "Are you okay?"

"It's so cold in here, Jaxon," Abby said. "I can't get the door open. Mr. Finnegan locked me in. When the boat shifted, I think something hit it and bent the doorframe."

Jaxon examined the area around the door and realized Abby was correct. The metal casing around the door was bent. "I'm going to get you out of there."

"You need to save yourself."

"I'm not leaving here without you."

"Jaxon . . . you don't have to do that," Abby said. "None of this is your fault."

Her words washed over him. It was like Abby knew the guilt Jaxon had been carrying, and she didn't want him to lug around any more of that culpability if something happened to her.

That was when he knew without a doubt that Abby was someone he wanted in his life for a long, long time.

That meant he had to get her out of there.

"How's it going?" Luke yelled.

"I need to figure out a way to get this door off," Jaxon said.

"Try this." Luke tossed him a crowbar.

As he did, another gunshot rang out.

"Backup is on the way," Luke said.

Jaxon shoved the crowbar into the door facing and used it to leverage the two pieces of the boat apart. It was working.

"Go get him," Jaxon said. "I've got this."

"You sure?" Luke asked.

"Positive."

He watched as his brother and the deputy jumped from the boat and sloshed through the water toward the woods.

Jaxon turned back to the door.

It was time to rescue the woman he was beginning to fall in love with.

ABBY'S LEGS were becoming numb, and her teeth chattered so bad they hurt. She'd never felt cold like this before. The water was up to her waist now. If she didn't get out of here soon, she'd be a goner.

She'd tried everything to open the door, but nothing worked.

"Jaxon?" she called, touching the door and wishing she could see him.

"Yes?"

She heard him doing something on the other side of the door, no doubt trying to get it open. Abby could picture it all playing out. She could see the determination on Jaxon's face.

"Thank you for everything that you've done for me." Her voice cracked.

"Don't talk like that."

"Talk like what?" She shivered. It was so cold in here that her bones throbbed.

How much longer could she survive these conditions?

"You sound like you're saying goodbye," Jaxon said. "Don't do that."

"I don't have much time left." Her teeth chattered. "I just want to let you know how much you have come to mean to me over the past few days. You went above and beyond to help me. I couldn't have asked God to send me anyone better in this situation."

"This isn't the end, Abby," Jaxon said.

As soon as he said the words, the boat shifted and Abby hit the wall again. More water rushed in, this time soaking her hair. She drew in a frosty breath and felt the cold enter her lungs.

"Abby, are you okay?" Jaxon shouted.

"I'm fine. I just need you to know how much I appreciate you. Just in case . . . you know. I don't deserve another chance at love—"

"I beg to differ," Jaxon said. "I know you don't think you deserve all the good things in life that you have coming to you, but you're wrong. You do. Just because someone fooled you, doesn't mean you should be punished for the rest of your life."

"I don't know if I can ever forgive myself, though." Tears wanted to come, but she was fresh out.

"You can, Abby. I know you can."

Just as he said the words, Abby felt the door move.

Her breath caught. Had Jaxon figured something out?

The next instant, light flooded the stairwell. The

bottom of the door peeled back. He'd pried it open, hadn't he?

Jaxon's face appeared in the opening.

"Abby . . . come on." He reached for her.

The whole door hadn't opened, only part of it had been bent back. She reached for him, barely able to move. Her body felt numb. Weak. Uncontrollable.

But that was okay. Because Jaxon was here. His arms wrapped around Abby, and he pulled her from her watery grave.

The next instant, more police boats pulled up. Men boarded the watercraft, and a blanket was thrown around her shoulders.

"It's going to be okay." Jaxon cradled her in his arms. "It's going to be okay."

CHAPTER FORTY-THREE

JAXON HADN'T LEFT Abby's side since he'd rescued her from the sinking boat. Luke and his deputy had arrested Ron Finnegan, and he was now in custody. From what Jaxon understood, the man had also killed Theresa and Kathy Turner—their first victim here in Fog Lake—as well as those other women in Minnesota.

Apparently, Theresa had been meeting with an old high school boyfriend during the month before she died. Ron Finnegan decided Theresa needed justice for her indiscretions.

Now knowing what he did about Mr. Finnegan's past, the pieces came together. A sick and twisted picture formed, but Jaxon could see the pattern of women messing up Mr. Finnegan's life, at least from a madman's perspective.

Jaxon was just happy because Abby was here with him and she was okay. She had warming blankets on her now. Other than the hypothermia and some rope burns on her wrists and ankles, she appeared to be fine. But things could have turned out so much differently.

Jaxon reached across the hospital bed and squeezed her hand. Neither of them had to say anything to communicate what they were feeling.

Abby cleared her throat. "How's Cait Kovach? I haven't been able to stop thinking about the detective since I regained consciousness."

"She's in stable condition," Jaxon said. "The doctor said he thinks she's going to pull through."

"That's great news."

"And Will Able, the attorney from the diner, was cleared. He wasn't a part of any of this."

"That's good to know." Abby took a sip of her water through the little plastic straw in the Styrofoam cup. "Tell me about the man you took off chasing at the Hills, Hollows, and Hearts."

"You won't believe me if I tell you." Jaxon crossed his arms and raised his eyebrows.

"Try me. I've had some pretty unbelievable things happen to me recently."

"I can't argue with that. It turns out he was with the CIA."

Abby's eyes widened. "Okay, that is a little unbelievable."

He shrugged. "I'm telling the truth, though. He showed me his badge and gave me his card. While the doctor was checking you out, I even called to check his credentials."

"And?"

"It appears that he's legit."

"What did he want with you?"

"He said the CIA has been keeping an eye on me since I got out of the military. They're interested in hiring me."

Abby's eyes widened, but not particularly with excitement. He had trouble reading the emotion there. "Wow. That has to be flattering."

"If I work for the CIA, I'm going to be in more situations just like the one I faced in Iraq. I can't do that."

"Or you could be the change. You could be the compassionate one who sticks to his moral compass."

Jaxon shook his head. "I'm done with that kind of

life. I need to reconnect with my family."

"So you think you'll be sticking around here?"

"I want to give the coffee business a go. See what happens. You never know unless you try, right?"

She squeezed his hand. "I think that sounds like a fantastic idea."

He looked at her, at the lovely angles of her face. Even in the hospital room, she looked gorgeous. Not many people could pull that off. He hated to think about her leaving.

"How about you?" he asked. "Are you going to go back to Georgia?"

"I'm really not sure what there is for me there, other than Renee. I know I'm going to go back there and see how she's doing. She's going to need some support after losing her husband. Do you think that was connected with what happened here?"

Jaxon felt his muscles tighten. "I know that Luke is still talking to Mr. Finnegan, but from what I gather, Ron was trying to get information from Renee about where you were. We do believe that the incidents are connected."

Another cry escaped from Abby. Jaxon knew this was a lot for her to handle, and that it would take some time for her to work through everything.

"I'm so sorry that all this has happened to you,

Abby." He lowered his voice.

"Thank you. Me too." Her gaze latched onto his. "But you know what? I was thinking that once I go home and get everything settled with my business and my dad and Renee . . . I was thinking that they might need a bakery here in Fog Lake."

A light spread in his eyes. "How about a bakery and coffeehouse?"

Her eyebrows shot up. "You're thinking about buying it?"

"The thought crossed my mind. But I would need just the right partner. What do you think?"

A grin stretched across her lips. "I think it sounds like a great idea."

He rubbed the sides of her arms and stared into her eyes. His voice sounded low as he said, "Once you get out of the hospital and get everything settled, maybe we'll talk then."

"I think that sounds like a great idea." Abby smiled. "Thanks, Jaxon. For everything."

"No, thank you, Abby. You helped me see that I still have a lot left to give in this life."

He bent forward until his lips touched her hand.

Sometimes, the hardest times in life brought about the most beautiful moments. This was one of them.

CHAPTER FORTY-FOUR

ABBY FELT herself beaming as she opened the door and Jaxon's family flooded inside Fog Lake's newest business.

She grinned. "Welcome to The Busy Bean."

Murmurs of excitement followed a round of compliments as everyone paused on the wood floors and glanced around the newly renovated, newly named coffeehouse.

"It looks great in here." Ansley nodded and plucked up a chocolate chip cookie.

"And it smells heavenly," Harper added.

"I'm excited for you guys," Luke said. "I think this is going to be great. We have a new hangout now."

"Free coffee for life!" Boone added.

Jaxon squeezed her hand. Abby had come back

to Fog Lake three months ago. She'd moved in with Ansley, who'd been looking for a roommate. But Ansley would be getting married in six months.

When she did, Abby's friend Renee was going to move to Fog Lake too. Renee felt like she needed a new start, and this area seemed like just the place to recover for her grieving heart after everything that had happened.

A person at the very end of the line caught Abby's attention. She reached out her arms and pulled Jaxon's mom, Elise, into a hug. "I'm so glad that you came."

"I'm so glad that you invited me. Thank you all."

Over the past six months, Jaxon's mom had been doing more and more things with the family. Slowly but surely, they were starting to warm up to her, and a new kind of normal was forming between them. Abby couldn't be happier.

Meanwhile, Ron Finnegan was in jail for two counts of murder, two counts of abduction, plus numerous other charges. He wouldn't be getting out in this lifetime.

Abby hadn't heard from Patrick in a long time. That was a good thing. He may not have been guilty of killing his wife, but he still wasn't the kind of person that Abby wanted to be in touch with. He had a lot of growing up to do, to say the least.

Harper had worked with Abby and connected her with some reputable reporters. Abby's version of what had happened in her relationship with Patrick had aired two months ago. Speculation about her reputation seemed to be settling down. She was forever grateful for Harper's help in getting her story out. Maybe other people could learn from her experiences.

Dirk Watson had even endorsed Jaxon's coffee brand. That, mixed with Abby's baked goods, seemed to be the recipe for success. If nothing else, Jaxon and Abby enjoyed working together. They made a good team.

Jaxon leaned closer, his breath tickling her ear. "I love you, Abby Brennan."

Warmth spread through her. "I love you too, Jaxon."

Luke tapped on the side of a coffee mug with a spoon until everyone turned their attention on him. Abby stepped closer to Jaxon and waited to hear what he had to say.

"I just wanted to let you all know some good news," Luke said. "Harper and I are expecting!"

More rounds of hugs and congratulations went around.

This place wasn't perfect. Not by any means. But it felt like home, and it had a charm and a lore all of its own. There was no other place that Abby would rather be. Especially when she had Jaxon by her side.

ALSO BY CHRISTY BARRITT:

Edge of Peril

When evil descends like fog on a mountain community, no one feels safe. After hearing about a string of murders in a Smoky Mountain town, journalist Harper Jennings realizes a startling truth. She knows who may be responsible—the same person who tried to kill her three years ago. Now Harper must convince the cops to believe her before the killer strikes again. Sheriff Luke Wilder returned to his hometown, determined to keep the promise he made to his dying father. The sleepy tourist area with a tragic past hadn't seen a murder in decades—until now. Keeping the community safe seems impossible as darkness edges closer, threatening to consume everything in its path. As The Watcher grows desperate, Harper and Luke must work together in order to defeat him. But the peril around them escalates, making it clear the killer will stop at nothing to get what he wants.

Margin of Error

Some secrets have deadly consequences. Brynlee Parker thought her biggest challenge would be hiking to Dead Man's Bluff and fulfilling her dad's last wishes. She never thought she'd witness two men being viciously murdered while on a mountainous trail. Even worse, the deadly predator is now hunting her. Boone Wilder wants nothing to do with Dead Man's Bluff, not after his wife died there. But he can't seem to mind his own business when a mysterious out-of-towner burst into his camp store in a frenzied panic. Something—or someone—deadly is out there. The killer's hunger for blood seems to be growing at a brutal pace. Can Brynlee and Boone figure out who's behind these murders? Or will the hurts and secrets from their past not allow for even a margin of error?

Brink of Danger

Ansley Wilder has always lived life on the wild side, using thrills to numb the pain from her past and escape her mistakes. But a near-death experience two years ago changed everything. When another incident nearly claims her life, she turns her thrill-seeking ways into a fight for survival. Ryan Philips left Fog Lake to chase adventure far from home. Now he's returned as the new fire chief in town, but the slower paced life he seeks is nowhere to be found. Not only is a wildfire blazing out of control, but a malicious killer known as "The Woodsman" is enacting crimes that appear accidental. Plus, there seems to be a strange connection with these incidents and his best friend's little sister, Ansley Wilder. As a killer watches their every move and the forest fire threatens to destroy their scenic town, both Ryan and Ansley hover on the brink of danger. One wrong move could send them tumbling over the edge . . . permanently.

YOU ALSO MIGHT LIKE:

LANTERN BEACH MYSTERIES

Hidden Currents

You can take the detective out of the investigation, but you can't take the investigator out of the detective. A notorious gang puts a bounty on Detective Cady Matthews's head after she takes down their leader, leaving her no choice but to hide until she can testify at trial. But her temporary home across the country on a remote North Carolina island isn't as peaceful as she initially thinks. Living under the new identity of Cassidy Livingston, she struggles to keep her investigative skills tucked away, especially after a body washes ashore. When local police bungle the murder investigation, she can't resist stepping in. But Cassidy is supposed to be keeping a low profile. One wrong move could lead to both her discovery and her demise. Can she bring justice to the island . . . or will the hidden currents surrounding her pull her under for good?

Flood Watch

The tide is high, and so is the danger on Lantern Beach. Still in hiding after infiltrating a dangerous gang, Cassidy Livingston just has to make it a few more months before she can testify at trial and resume her old life. But trouble keeps finding her, and Cassidy is pulled into a local investigation after a man mysteriously disappears from the island she now calls home. A recurring nightmare from her time undercover only muddies things, as does a visit from the parents of her handsome ex-Navy SEAL neighbor. When a friend's life is threatened, Cassidy must make choices that put her on the verge of blowing her cover. With a flood watch on her emotions and her life in a tangle, will Cassidy find the truth? Or will her past finally drown her?

Storm Surge

A storm is brewing hundreds of miles away, but its effects are devastating even from afar. Laid-back, loose, and light: that's Cassidy Livingston's new motto. But when a makeshift boat with a bloody cloth inside washes ashore near her oceanfront home, her detective instincts shift into gear . . . again. Seeking clues isn't the only thing on her mind—romance is heating up with next-door neighbor and former Navy SEAL Ty Chambers as well. Her heart wants the love and stability she's longed for her entire life. But her hidden identity only leads to a tidal wave of turbulence. As more answers emerge about the boat, the danger around her rises, creating a treacherous swell that threatens to reveal her past. Can Cassidy mind her own business, or will the storm surge of violence and corruption that has washed ashore on Lantern Beach leave her life in wreckage?

Dangerous Waters

Danger lurks on the horizon, leaving only two choices: find shelter or flee. Cassidy Livingston's new identity has begun to feel as comfortable as her favorite sweater. She's been tucked away on Lantern Beach for weeks, waiting to testify against a deadly gang, and is settling in to a new life she wants to last

forever. When she thinks she spots someone malev-
olent from her past, panic swells inside her. If an
enemy has found her, Cassidy won't be the only one
who's a target. Everyone she's come to love will also
be at risk. Dangerous waters threaten to pull her into
an overpowering chasm she may never escape. Can
Cassidy survive what lies ahead? Or has the tide
fatally turned against her?

Perilous Riptide

Just when the current seems safer, an unseen
danger emerges and threatens to destroy everything.
When Cassidy Livingston finds a journal hidden
deep in the recesses of her ice cream truck, her
curiosity kicks into high gear. Islanders suspect that
Elsa, the journal's owner, didn't die accidentally. Her
final entry indicates their suspicions might be
correct and that what Elsa observed on her final
night may have led to her demise. Against the advice
of Ty Chambers, her former Navy SEAL boyfriend,
Cassidy taps into her detective skills and hunts for
answers. But her search only leads to a skeletal body
and trouble for both of them. As helplessness
threatens to drown her, Cassidy is desperate to turn
back time. Can Cassidy find what she needs to navigate the perilous situation? Or will the riptide

surrounding her threaten everyone and everything Cassidy loves?

Deadly Undertow

The current's fatal pull is powerful, but so is one detective's will to live. When someone from Cassidy Livingston's past shows up on Lantern Beach and warns her of impending peril, opposing currents collide, threatening to drag her under. Running would be easy. But leaving would break her heart. Cassidy must decipher between the truth and lies, between reality and deception. Even more importantly, she must decide whom to trust and whom to fear. Her life depends on it. As danger rises and answers surface, everything Cassidy thought she knew is tested. In order to survive, Cassidy must take drastic measures and end the battle against the ruthless gang DH-7 once and for all. But if her final mission fails, the consequences will be as deadly as the raging undertow.

LANTERN BEACH ROMANTIC SUSPENSE

Tides of Deception

Change has come to Lantern Beach: a new police chief, a new season, and . . . a new romance? Austin

Brooks has loved Skye Lavinia from the moment they met, but the walls she keeps around her seem impenetrable. Skye knows Austin is the best thing to ever happen to her. Yet she also knows that if he learns the truth about her past, he'd be a fool not to run. A chance encounter brings secrets bubbling to the surface, and danger soon follows. Are the life-threatening events plaguing them really accidents . . . or is someone trying to send a deadly message? With the tides on Lantern Beach come deception and lies. One question remains—who will be swept away as the water shifts? And will it bring the end for Austin and Skye, or merely the beginning?

Shadow of Intrigue

For her entire life, Lisa Garth has felt like a supporting character in the drama of life. The designation never bothered her—until now. Lantern Beach, where she's settled and runs a popular restaurant, has boarded up for the season. The slower pace leaves her with too much time alone. Braden Dillinger came to Lantern Beach to try to heal. The former Special Forces officer returned from battle with invisible scars and diminished hope. But his recovery is hampered by the fact that an unknown enemy is trying to kill him. From the moment Lisa and Braden meet, danger ignites around them, and both are drawn into a web of intrigue that turns their lives upside down. As shadows creep in, will Lisa and Braden be able to shine a light on the peril around them? Or will the encroaching darkness turn their worst nightmares into reality?

Storm of Doubt

A pastor who's lost faith in God. A romance writer who's lost faith in love. A faceless man with a deadly obsession. Nothing has felt right in Pastor Jack Wilson's world since his wife died two years ago. He hoped coming to Lantern Beach might help soothe the ragged edges of his soul. Instead, he feels more alone than ever. Novelist Juliette Grace came to the island to hide away. Though her professional life has never been better, her personal life has imploded. Her husband left her and a stalker's threats have grown more and more dangerous. When Jack saves Juliette from an attack, he sees the terror in her gaze and knows he must protect her. But when danger strikes again, will Jack be able to keep her safe? Or will the approaching storm prove too strong to withstand?

Winds of Danger

Wes O'Neill is perfectly content to hang with his friends and enjoy island life on Lantern Beach. Something begins to change inside him when Paige Henderson sweeps into his life. But the beautiful newcomer is hiding painful secrets beneath her cheerful facade. Police dispatcher Paige Henderson came to Lantern Beach riddled with guilt and uncertainties after the fallout of a bad relationship. When she meets Wes, she begins to open up to the possibility of love again. But there's something Wes isn't telling her—something that could change everything. As the winds shift, doubts seep into Paige's mind. Can Paige and Wes trust each other, even as the currents work against them? Or is trouble from the past too much to overcome?

LANTERN BEACH PD

On the Lookout

When Cassidy Chambers accepted the job as police chief on Lantern Beach, she knew the island had its secrets. But a suspicious death with potentially far-reaching implications will test all her skills —and threaten to reveal her true identity. Cassidy enlists the help of her husband, former Navy SEAL

Ty Chambers. As they dig for answers, both uncover parts of their pasts that are best left buried. Not everything is as it seems, and they must figure out if their John Doe is connected to the secretive group that has moved onto the island. As facts materialize, danger on the island grows. Can Cassidy and Ty discover the truth about the shadowy crimes in their cozy community? Or has darkness permanently invaded their beloved Lantern Beach?

Attempt to Locate

A fun girls' night out turns into a nightmare when armed robbers barge into the store where Cassidy and her friends are shopping. As the situation escalates and the men escape, a massive manhunt launches on Lantern Beach to apprehend the dangerous trio. In the midst of the chaos, a potential foe asks for Cassidy's help. He needs to find his sister who fled from the secretive Gilead's Cove community on the island. But the more Cassidy learns about the seemingly untouchable group, the more her unease grows. The pressure to solve both cases continues to mount. But as the gravity of the situation rises, so does the danger. Cassidy is determined to protect the island and break up the cult . . . but doing so might cost her everything.

First Degree Murder

Police Chief Cassidy Chambers longs for a break from the recent crimes plaguing Lantern Beach. She simply wants to enjoy her friends' upcoming wedding, to prepare for the busy tourist season about to slam the island, and to gather all the dirt she can on the suspicious community that's invaded the town. But trouble explodes on the island, sending residents—including Cassidy—into a squall of uneasiness. Cassidy may have more than one enemy plotting her demise, and the collateral damage seems unthinkable. As the temperature rises, so does the pressure to find answers. Someone is determined that Lantern Beach would be better off without their new police chief. And for Cassidy, one wrong move could mean certain death.

Dead on Arrival

With a highly charged local election consuming the community, Police Chief Cassidy Chambers braces herself for a challenging day of breaking up petty conflicts and tamping down high emotions. But when widespread food poisoning spreads among potential voters across the island, Cassidy smells something rotten in the air. As Cassidy examines every possibility to uncover what's going on, local enigma Anthony Gilead again comes on her radar. The man is running for mayor and his cult-like following is growing at an alarming rate. Cassidy feels certain he has a spy embedded in her inner circle. The problem is that her pool of suspects gets deeper every day. Can Cassidy get to the bottom of what's eating away at her peaceful island home? Will voters turn out despite the outbreak of illness plaguing their tranquil town? And the even bigger question: Has darkness come to stay on Lantern Beach?

Plan of Action

A missing Navy SEAL. Danger at the boiling point. The ultimate showdown. When Police Chief Cassidy Chambers' husband, Ty, disappears, her world is turned upside down. His truck is discovered with blood inside, crashed in a ditch on Lantern Beach, but he's nowhere to be found. As they launch a manhunt to find him, Cassidy discovers that someone on the island has a deadly obsession with Ty. Meanwhile, Gilead's Cove seems to be imploding. As danger heightens, federal law enforcement officials are called in. The cult's growing threat could lead to the pinnacle standoff of good versus evil. A clear plan of action is needed or the results will be devastating. Will Cassidy find Ty in time, or will she face a gut-wrenching loss? Will Anthony Gilead finally be unmasked for who he really is and be brought to justice? Hundreds of innocent lives are at stake . . . and not everyone will come out alive.

THE SQUEAKY CLEAN MYSTERY SERIES

On her way to completing a degree in forensic science, Gabby St. Claire drops out of school and starts her own crime-scene cleaning business. When a routine cleaning job uncovers a murder weapon the police overlooked, she realizes that the wrong person is in jail. She also realizes that crime scene cleaning might be the perfect career for utilizing her investigative skills.

#1 Hazardous Duty

#2 Suspicious Minds

#2.5 It Came Upon a Midnight Crime (novella)

#3 Organized Grime

#4 Dirty Deeds

#5 The Scum of All Fears

When Holly Anna Paladin is given a year to live, she embraces her final days doing what she loves most—random acts of kindness. But when one of her extreme good deeds goes horribly wrong, implicating Holly in a string of murders, Holly is suddenly in a different kind of fight for her life. She knows one thing for sure: she only has a short amount of time to make a difference. And if helping the people she cares about puts her in danger, it's a risk worth taking.

#1 Random Acts of Murder
#2 Random Acts of Deceit
#2.5 Random Acts of Scrooge

THE WORST DETECTIVE EVER:

I'm not really a private detective. I just play one on TV.

Joey Darling, better known to the world as Raven Remington, detective extraordinaire, is trying to separate herself from her invincible alter ego. She played the spunky character for five years on the hit TV show *Relentless*, which catapulted her to fame and into the role of Hollywood's sweetheart. When her marriage falls apart, her finances dwindle to nothing, and her father disappears, Joey finds herself on the Outer Banks of North Carolina, trying to piece together her life away from the limelight. But as people continually mistake her for the character she played on TV, she's tasked with solving real life crimes . . . even though she's terrible at it.

ABOUT THE AUTHOR

USA Today has called Christy Barritt's books "scary, funny, passionate, and quirky."

Christy writes both mystery and romantic suspense novels that are clean with underlying messages of faith. Her books have won the Daphne du Maurier Award for Excellence in Suspense and Mystery, have been twice nominated for the Romantic Times Reviewers' Choice Award, and have finaled for both a Carol Award and Foreword Magazine's Book of the Year.

She is married to her Prince Charming, a man who thinks she's hilarious—but only when she's not trying to be. Christy is a self-proclaimed klutz, an avid music lover who's known for spontaneously bursting into song, and a road trip aficionado.

When she's not working or spending time with her family, she enjoys singing, playing the guitar, and exploring small, unsuspecting towns where people have no idea how accident-prone she is.

Find Christy online at:
www.christybarritt.com
www.facebook.com/christybarritt
www.twitter.com/cbarritt

Sign up for Christy's newsletter to get information on all of her latest releases here: **www. christybarritt.com/newsletter-sign-up/**

If you enjoyed this book, please consider leaving a review.